# Toasted Ravioli

# Toasted Ravioli

### Compiled by
P. Anthony Mast

### Cover design and Photography by
Den Dotson and Colleen Dempsey Dotson

Published by: The St. Louis Writers Meetup Group

Printed by: lulu.com

ISBN: 978-0-6151-7027-5

For more information, please visit:

www.toastedraviolibook.com

# Table of Contents

# In Thanks

Den Dotson –

"Dedicated first, to my lovely wife, Colleen, who gives up time with her husband to give the world a new writer. Second, to a great friend, Kevin Brown, who believes I can write and believes it enough to edit my work, a labor of pure love. And last, to the great folks of the St. Louis Writers Meetup, you folks inspire, astound, and somedays confound me."


Joshua Ebling –

"To my mother, for her love, and support.
To Toni, and Tony, for their edits, and my writing group for putting up with my truancy with the deadline.
And finally, to the cute, short haired brunette that inspired the story."

Marqua McGull –

"To:

Raigan Billingsley, my daughter, without whose love, I would write without purpose;

Keith McGull, my brother, without whose love, I would write without challenge; Barbara and the late Raymond McGull, without whose love and guidance, I would be without character.


Acknowledgements:

To my family Martine, Jaelin, Raymond and Jean McGull; Bobbie, Whitney and Bryce Billingsley, and Rashonda Dillard for all their love and encouragement;

To my dear friends Brenda Williams, Karin Fowler, Elise Humphrey, Chanda Woods, Deborah Howard, Diane Irving, Toni Whitfield, Wayne Owens and Terrence Hamilton, who have always been there for me;

To Jon and Verlean Nicks of Legacy Books (St. Louis, MO)  and Reverend Johnnie Scott, NAACP (E. St. Louis,IL) for believing in my writing without hesitation, and Reverend Earl Nance, Jr. and the Greater Mt. Carmel Baptist Church, for feeding the spiritual needs of this writer; who fed the spiritual needs of this writer.

To my Wednesday night crew, Melvin, Henry, Columbus, Beverly, William, Monica, Keith, John, Randy, Pamela, Valerie, Arbary, LaLa, Sy, Chucky, Dennis and all of the rollers at Skate King Roller Rink, for just being my friends!


Special Acknowledgment:

To the memory of the late Jerry F. Baker, who taught how life should be lived in the face of death."

Jane Wallace Reed –

"I would like to dedicate all of my writings in this book to my parents, Sally Givens Aton McCormick and George Frank McCormick, as well as all the wonderful teachers in my life, who taught me to how to think, and how to love learning for its own sake."


Mike Beckett –

"To Michelle, the only person with enough patience to marry a spaz like me.

And to Tony Mast, in the hopes that he won't fulfill his promise to kill us all when this anthology is finished.

And finally, to my dog Molly, without whom my story would not have happened."


Jennifer Shew –

"This is dedicated to my parents, who took me to the Muny when I was little, and claim they are not at all biased when they praise what I write.

I'd also like to acknowledge all the wonderful fantasy authors out there who give my imagination a workout and inspire me to be a better writer. I can only hope that one day I can be like you."


P. Anthony Mast Jr. –

"I dedicate this work to Julie and Holden, my wife and son. I also dedicate this to the dream that is growing inside of Julie as I write this."

# FOREWORD

Thank you!

Thank you for purchasing this book or even flipping through it and finding this.

In January of 2006, the St. Louis Writers Meetup Group had been gathering for about a year and the group had settled into a collection of 8 to 10 individuals who were semi-regular participants in the monthly meetings. It was around this time that a twist of chance placed me in the position of Organizer of the group. I had been making leaps forward in my writing, as had many of the other members of our group.

At our meeting that month, I presented an idea to the rest of the group. We were going to self-publish an anthology.

The theme of the anthology isn't too far from any of those who contributed to it. It's the place we live. We are an amazing, diverse collection of individuals whose different styles and subjects are representative of the city we call home. St. Louis is a town rich in history and culture. We hope that we have captured some of that in this book.

It is over 18 months later, and the book is, for all intents, done.

It has been a long, strange road to get to this point. We've had members of the group come and go, stories change and revert back, and new projects start and others end. Lives are different and this book is a snapshot of our lives and our writing.

Though the only place you'll see his name is in this introduction, this book would not have been completed without the work of Anthony Kuenzel. He helped push each of us in our writing. He also helped keep me motivated during the long hours of helping each writer craft their stories. His work should be in this book, and if you knew what to look for, you'd see it. But trust me, it's there.

Thank you again, and we hope that you enjoy our writings,

P. Anthony Mast Jr.

August 6, 2007

# Toasted Ravioli

# The Dutiful Kill

By Marqua McGull

October 28, 1963

3:39 a.m.


It was the tale of the voodoo curse that started us, Grandfather Caleb and I, into the darkness of the St. Louis riverfront. We stumbled along wet and algae laden cobblestones until we stood as two destined souls on firm, moist ground outside a gigantic warehouse. Metal doors, triple wide, separated us from everything within. Humid morning air, smelling of fish, ensconced us with stifling warmth like that of a woolen blanket, yet I trembled in my shoes. My freshly ironed tee shirt, wilted from sweat and humidity, clung to my skin.

Caleb's small, strong frame, stooped naturally from old age, leaned downward. In his left hand, he grasped a .12 gauge pump shotgun. Its weight pulled him like a magnet, drawing him even closer to the ground. And I had not, until this very moment, honestly appreciated that once we were inside the building, Caleb planned to kill everything in our path.

His murderous intent and my obvious fear melded, creating a lasting and frightening mental scenario of the two of us, for the remainder of our lives, peering from behind steel bars of the state penitentiary. At the sheer thought of the image, my nerves jump-started into a jerky electric trot up and down my body.

I was younger and of significant size, recruited solely, as Caleb had been, because I had been born the oldest male of my generation. My only task required me to help him escape the mayhem he was prepared to cause. So, at his vehement insistence, I had promised to not interfere.

The lapping waters of the Mississippi churned with monotonous gurgles as the muddy liquid calmly declared the life story of the great river. A transparent layer of mist clothed the murky waters and drifted east over the Illinois landscape. Though Caleb knew thoroughly the layout of the silent warehouse, as if it had suddenly transformed unfamiliar to him, he looked up and down the facade of the massive building; in odd unison, I mimicked his movement.

He then turned his attention to view the few remaining dilapidated buildings on the riverfront, which in times past had been shelter to open and vibrant businesses, noisy and alive with river trade, but now dead and closed. A smile crept across his shriveled, brown lips, perhaps the effect of our absolute oasis and the quiet before the tempestuous storm, though I would never learn what had amused him.

Suddenly, the two boxes of double naught buckshot he gripped under his left armpit loosened. With the swiftness of an animal trap locking onto its prey, he clasped the boxes tighter and regained control. The activity prompted him to return to the matter at hand, for he had things to do, a schedule to keep, souls to release and a people to save. Caleb pulled the boxes closer to his left side and unfolded his back to stand as tall as he could get. Time was not to be wasted. He raised his right hand to the operating panel alongside the wide door and moved the lever; the door awakened.

We listened as metal clicked from the door's mechanism. Amid the cacophony of scraping mechanical noises, Caleb spoke. "Yeah, I know you young un' don't b'lieve me- ya' think mine's da' ramblins' of a crazy ol' man, but, I know what I know, an' I ain't a scared of it, nah, I ain't!"

As the door opened, its moaning sounds drowned out the hypnotic sounds from the deep waters of the river.

Together, we slipped from the night's natural darkness, across the threshold, into an eerie blackness. Past the door's opening, we crept into the gaping vastness of the huge warehouse; it felt remarkably cool. Thankfully,

Caleb's insistence that the building did not have an alarm proved correct. We walked deeper inside.

Behind us, as if on its own cue, the door quietly lowered itself closed, flush against the concrete floor, sealing us instantly inside the bowels so tightly that not a draft of humidity stirred where the door met the ground. Neither of us uttered a word. An inky darkness encircled us. Inside, the sound of total quiet allowed only the passing of time to be heard.

After a few seconds as if ushered in by the stagnant warmth, an awful smell rushed upon us, crowding into our nostrils. For a few seconds, Caleb stirred about, batting at the smell. It would be to no avail for the smell remained intense. I sensed he knew the futility of his gestures for he calmed down and cleared his throat, disturbing the silence. A soulful prayer followed.

"Lawd, please bless'n us, even if we doin' wrong tonight. An' let it stay wid' us fo' we doin' dis' to save our people."

A lump formed inside my throat whereby I could not swallow; I rubbed my neck.

After the prayer, he reached into the deep front pocket of his flannel work shirt, thinning from years of usage, and pulled out a flashlight; it would be our only source of light. Earlier, Caleb had explained that any more light would be unnecessary because the jaundiced hue from behind the eyes of the monsters would be his targets. At that time, I had discounted the seriousness of the statement. He flicked it on. Unable to pierce the deep darkness, the light from the flashlight spilled in front of us and became lost no more than two feet ahead.

"That doesn't work, I still can't see!"

"Don't you worry 'bout us havin' no good light, jus' look real good at they eyes and you'll see that pee yellow light behind 'em, that's all the light we gone need. Dey' eyes show the evil. And don't worry, they only come alive when a whole lot of people together, jus' the two of us ain't gone give 'em enough strength."

Streams of sweat rolled down my back. I swallowed the lump.

Without warning, Caleb thrust the flashlight into my hand, which I gladly accepted because I needed to feel that I was in control of at least something in this venture. The inky darkness erased my hand. I turned the light onto his face. Deep wrinkles folded about his gentle brown face. My emotions welled inside at the thought of this old man risking his life to accept the bequest of the legend that, for the past five generations, had been bestowed upon the oldest male of my family.

Caleb looked upward, his rheumy eyes set in a deep intelligent stare. I pointed the light in the direction of his gaze, illuminating the ceiling high above. Inexplicably, the same ray of light, moments earlier having been fettered by the darkness, now shone remarkably deep and bright. I could not believe what I saw. Before I knew it, the word slipped from my mouth.

"Damn!"

Caleb chuckled at my anxiety.

There it stood, a gigantic dragon, sapphire in color! Caleb and I gazed into the black pupils of the savagery, each one painted center inside a pair of crimson glass eyes the size of tennis balls. Its eye sockets set poised high above the massive snout of its enormous head. A long emerald tongue, snarled angrily past keen, saw-like yellow teeth. The ferocious monster reared back on a thick tail and stood three stories tall, at least, its two short forearms scratching at the air. Made from mounds and mounds of papier-mâché, many layers of brush stroked paint created the illusion of rippled skin.

Two other dragons of the same material, one black and the other green, stood locked in savage battle with each other. They were each half the size of the blue monster. The menagerie of wild beasts perched harmlessly on top of a parade float. And behind the dragons, deeper inside the warehouse, the blurry silhouettes of many other figures shadowed the walls - comic strip characters, figurines and characters on each float. Every character represented a popular image, from southern minstrel shows and local store mannequins, to fable and mythological characters, various storybook and comedy characters, all vintage and molded setting atop fifteen floats.

I heard clearly his movements. The spill of the light permitted me to see him adjust the huge shotgun and fumble with the two boxes of shells. With the countenance of a mad scientist about to engage in an earth shattering experiment, his short legs carried him confidently closer to his quarry. Likewise, I stepped with him. My heart pounded against my chest. I pointed the flashlight onto his face, back again at the dragons and then back to his face.

In my head, memories from conversations at family reunions and gatherings flashed. I recalled stories of how Grandpa Caleb, his father and grandfather had been known all over St. Louis. Tales were told of the old days, when Caleb's grandfather Abram, who lived on Second Street, so close to this warehouse that he could walk here everyday and take care of these creatures, to Caleb, who came from the Ville and the Mill Creek area up to the edge of town where white people lived. Up until this very moment, in succession of one another, great, great Grandfather Abram, Caleb's father, Caleb and my deceased father had all been the trusted caretakers, the only men, black or white, who knew the ins and outs and all the secrets behind the oldest annual affair of the vintage genteel society of St. Louis, the Veiled Prophet Parade. I shook my head at the weight of the burden my family carried.

In a low deep tone, he warned me. "I need ya' to git ready, ya' might wanna' cov'a yo' ears."

Fear forced me to try reasoning with the old man, this one last time, before he set about a course of action the two of us would never be able to explain. Words rose in my throat.

"Grandpa, I know what you've said all these years. But, let's wait a minute and..." However, before I could finish my plea, he offered his explanation.

"Naw, naw! Cause if I don't stop these monsters now, what you think gone happen to our people? All these years, my granddaddy Abram, since he was ten years old, Lawd bless his soul, and every' oldest man born thereafter, been the caretaker of these monsters. When Abram become the unwillin' servant of old Colonel Slayban and when he was brought to St. Louis, and he stotted' havin' chillun', Abram been tellin' the oldest boy of every generation that the Colonel di'int know what he bought and we gotta' protec' our people from the monsters cause our fam'ly been the only caretakers."

"Grandpa, I still say those old tales your grandfather Abram told you were just old superstitions."

"Why, evah since the old colonel got the idea back in 1878 to buy these creatures from the people over at the Mardi Gras, Abram been knowin' the secret and it wunt no supastition. These creatures is possessed, like they always been, from the voodoo put on 'em by the ole Negro witches that knowed how to punish white folk for bein' so hateful and mean to our people. Why the way granddaddy used to tell me and my daddy, our people couldn't even go too close to the Mardi Gras 'cause they was Negroes and the old women made 'em pay for they hatred. 'Dey made the creatures intah' soul snatchers!"

"So, if they're such creatures, then we can't really protect anyone, I mean, if there is really a curse, why have you and the others been able to take care of them for so long?"

He answered in a whisper, "The reason is real secret, and I been tole' it got somthin' to do with that magic. See, the runaway slaves hid amongst the Indians in Lou'siana and my grandpappy tole me that that magic was part Indian magic, they worked togetha'! From them Indians in Lou'siana, them witches learned somethin' diffrunt',real diffrunt'. Why, that stuff mixed together was a powerful thang! I been tellin' you alla' time, an' durin' the Mardi Gras when the white folk stood close and the heat and scent of all those people mix togetha' and form one powerful release, tha' when the voodoo came alive and for a short time, the creatures can snatch the soul of anybody who looked into 'dose glass eyes. 'Da creatures snatched the people's souls and the people would all be dead by the time the next Mardi Gras came around. But nobody evuh could figga' out why, cause the creatures was smart and every death was at different times, and never connected to the timin' of th' Mardi Gras. 'Course the colored folk all knew about the creatures and didn't mind that the white folk didn't want 'em there."

"Well, if you are so sure about the voodoo, why don't you just tell someone, let the authorities know? They can then take care of the problem, in a much better way than we can."

His tone rose in indignation.

"Boy, who gon' believe an ol' colored man talkin' 'bout voodoo from ova' close to a hunded yeas'? Nobody. That's who. So, I gotta do dis, and now."

With determined movements, he snapped the shotgun open and pushed a shell into the chamber. Hoping to distract his resolve, I blurted another question; my voice cracked.

"I mean, how do you know that they are really evil? How do you really know? These things look completely harmless to me."

A brief silence floated that I dared not interrupt. He replied slowly, the meaning behind each word very clear.

"Cause when the creatures was brought here and put in the parade, my daddy told me the same thing happened, over and over again, yea' afta' yea'. Every yea' after the Veiled Prophet Parade, Abram would secretly read the newspaper and sometime pick up on a'ticles of people dying from sicknesses they had only a short time. He figgered that they had been to the parade and had they souls snatched and they became zombies, actin' crazy, outta' they minds and then dying. And because he was knowed by everybody in St. Louis, he could ask questions and git answers, and he learned that those dying people had went to the parade the year befo'.

So, ya' see, I gotta' do this cuz' I promise my granddaddy and my daddy that if our people ever start comin' an lookin' in the eyes, I'd stop the soul snatchers. And up till now, white folk been kept our people from even comin' to the parade, 'cause they been mean jus' like the white folks in New Orleans. But now, with this civil rights stuff, we doin' mo' stuff than we ever did befo' an' evry' year colored folk gittin' closa' and closa' to the parade, and pert' soon, they gone be possess'd jus' like white folk, an' I gotta' stop it, afta' all of these yea's I gotta' stop it!"

So, I had heard for the hundredth time that there were the souls of unsuspecting spectators for the last one hundred years inside each and every one of those characters brought from New Orleans, and this had gone on from before the floats were sold to Slayban until now. And nobody knew about it or how to stop the curse of the voodoo, except my ancestors and now me! My lips turned dry as sandpaper. I mumbled a silent prayer. I heard a deep breath escape from Caleb's lips. His slow drawl followed.

"It time boy."

The old man sidled closer to the float, sniffing the air like a young puppy sensing the presence of its mother. I watched him closely. Despite the darkness, my eyes followed every move the old man made.

The parade, scheduled to begin in approximately seventeen hours, required that by late evening the floats be removed from the warehouse. Therefore, the white parade officials would be here soon. Without further hesitation, he raised the shotgun and pointed at the first kill, the large blue dragon. I accepted more and more that the only salvageable part of this escapade would be our planned quick exit, for to discover Caleb at the scene of destruction holding a smoking gun would surely mean, for the both us, the end. He stood as a rock and aimed easily at the dragon's left eye. He squeezed the trigger.

Booom!

The noise from the gunfire felt as though someone had just exploded a cannon in my ears; it deafened me. Caleb struggled against the powerful recoil and ducked down, pulling me with him. Before the noise of the shotgun would cease resonating, a thick wet substance gushed and splattered out, small pieces of it striking my damp shirt. Shards of the dragon's destroyed eye fell to the hard floor.

Within a split second, a burst of smoke spewed from the left socket of the beast and traveled upwards toward the ceiling. Behind the smoke, a thunderous burst of piercing yelps and screams, like those of caged primates, escaped upward, reverberated throughout the building and bounced off the walls as wavering echoes.

As we cowered, Grandpa and I looked up, in the direction of the commotion. He pointed toward the ceiling.

"Ahhh, there 'dey go! Look boy' tha life of all those white people is comin' out it, jus' lissen' to 'em!

And as I raised my hands to cover my ears, all my activity stopped. An odor so unpleasant, so necrotic that my own breath reeked of it, surrounded us; I coughed. Dizziness rushed upon me and I shook it off. A layer of heavy warm air, laced with the smell of the decaying flesh floated in the air. I covered my nose. As the smell grew with intensity, Grandpa coughed violently, but managed to ignore his distress. His body shook as he grabbed and held onto me.

The screams continued to escape and rise to the ceiling, followed by another gush of white smoke that grew more visible, billowed up and spiraled downward in a descending path like that of a falling leaf. To my surprise, Caleb pulled me to my feet, while with his free hand, he fanned futilely at the smoke, displaying no pity for the monster's demise. Before we would stand completely, an enormous sound echoed throughout, snatching our attention.

I turned the flashlight toward the noise. We witnessed the huge dragon as it cracked along its seams. The enormous body separated and toppled over, crashing down, smashing into a thousand pieces skipping across the floor. The right eye belched from its socket and with a thud, fell onto the floor. It rolled hastily toward Grandpa's left foot and stopped short of touching his shoe.

I pointed the flashlight into its glare. Innumerable points of light from deep within the orbital refused to beg for mercy. I pointed the flashlight into its stare. Grandpa reloaded another shell into the hot chamber.

The eye dared the old man to complete his mission. He obliged and for the second time that morning, he aimed and pulled the trigger.

Booom!

It burst open. More screams lurched out, screeching upward throughout the warehouse. Remnants of the round glass lay smashed on the floor; the last point of illumination darted upward and vanished into the darkness. He reloaded.

Grandpa turned his aim at the two smaller dragons. He raised the shotgun and pointed at the black one. The dragon waited patiently for death. Behind each organ of sight, a glint of small light pulsated like the pounding of a heart submitted to death. Again, Grandpa squeezed the trigger.

Booom! Booom!

Without hesitation, he reloaded, firing rapidly into the green dragon.

Boom! Boom!

Screeching sounds, highly pitched and louder, rose up and bounced off the ceiling and spread throughout the building as raucous laughter from the insane. A plume of white smoke rose from the vacant orbs and spiraled to the floor.

I followed as he moved about the warehouse, approaching each float, raising the shotgun level to his sight. With each pull of the trigger, he grew more proficient, exhibiting the casual grace of a hired assassin, accustomed to and highly expectant of the level of destruction caused by the high-powered weapon. His movements flowed smoother, much more rapid and with new found precision. Each of his shots produced results as he aimed into the eyes of each of the vintage figures, firing the weapon repeatedly and with ease reloading again and again, until finally, all the creatures lay dead. And as he killed each one of them, the bodies of all the soul snatching creatures, from animal form to human form, large to small, imploded from the relinquishment of all those stolen souls raging up and then downward, splitting and crashing into fragments onto the floor.

5:30 a.m.

Finally, the last sounds of released agony had terminated. White smoke floated in tissue thin layers. The warehouse grew quiet. Caleb's destiny, determined at his birth, had been fulfilled by the final blast of his shotgun. The stress of the evening task weighed heavily upon him and I gingerly helped him to the door.

Though he radiated with a quiet dignity and satisfaction, his strength had been temporary, for he was a man spent. I pulled the weapon from his grip, folded the empty boxes and slid them into the waistband of my jeans. I next grabbed Grandpa under his left armpit and hurried from the building. We slipped along the cobblestones toward his old truck. Because I knew he could not object, I commandeered the driver's seat. He slumped forward on the passenger side, a wasted old man.

During the twelve-minute drive home, his eyes remained shut and his chest heaved heavily. I helped him from the truck and guided him up the stairs to his bedroom for some much-needed rest. He stretched across the bed and turned his back toward me. He uttered weakly, "Nah, don't fo'get to wake me."

I turned and crossed into the living room. Located in front of the television set, his easy chair looked inviting. I plopped down on the chair and looked out of the window. The backdrop of the early morning sunrise stretched across the horizon. I turned on the television and returned my attention to the dawn outside the window. I would wait for the breaking news.

7:27 p.m.

I awakened amidst the noise of the tenor sharp blasts of loud trumpets. I knew the source of the annoying noise. I rubbed my face and looked past the television. Outside the window, typical in the city's night sky, sparse random white starlight sprinkled the grey black sky. Sunrise had escaped into sunset. I glanced across the room and saw Grandpa had not moved from the position that I last saw him.

The hairs on the back of my neck reached out and rubbed against my tee shirt. I raced from the chair. As I approached the bed, my knees wobbled as I struggled against my lungs to force myself to breathe. I reached out and touched his armpit. I knew that the most exhaustive challenge Grandpa had accepted, had been a sense of duty. Suddenly, with the quickness of a match that is lit and suddenly burns away, I realized my grandfather had acted on a moral sense that went beyond his love for me and it had taken his life. Tears welled in my eyes.

Blasting noise recaptured my attention. I swiped the tears from my face and gathered enough strength to approach the television. I moved with the fear of a man being hunted. The music on the television grew painfully louder. Beads of sweat popped onto my forehead. Within my throat, a lump the size of an apple formed and slid into place. My heart pounded against my chest.

My distance from the television allowed me to see only blurred black and white images, yet a freakish fear settled within me that the past events had been unyielding to the natural order of life. As I blinked away the remaining tears, I moved closer to the television. On the screen, the unmistakable monstrous blue dragon stood defiant to the dutiful kill. Identical to how they stood when I last saw them, the two smaller dragons posted, having repositioned themselves at the rear of the sapphire behemoth. No signs of cracks or breakage of their papier-mâché exterior could be seen. Their eyes gleamed and glinted in the night. All the other creatures, earlier picked off with the precision of a skilled marksman, rode gallant atop their appointed floats. They all looked at me!

But, as I pulled my attention from the creatures, what I saw was even more frightening. Human gaiety consumed every corner of the television. Like random drops of black paint on white paper, more than a few of my people had pushed themselves to the front of the crowd and stood boldly immersed among hundreds of white people. And with the much deserved freedom of a people starving to exercise their rights to exist, they gazed happily into the eyes of the soul snatchers, triumphantly enjoying the mystifying attraction of the creatures of the Veiled Prophet Parade.

# Gold and Emerald

By Joshua Ebling

His head spun. His eyes fluttered.

Something caused him to breach the line between his dreams and the hard, unyielding floor of his hotel room.

His feet ached. His head throbbed. Several hours spent crammed in the backseat of a crowded minivan doing eighty down the highway while the girls in the front sang Japanese pop songs did little to improve his mood.

He hadn't planned on going on the trip. He figured it would be worth the impending discomfort to go to the convention with his friends. This one was renowned for their Masquerade.

Ever since high school drama class, he'd always wanted to perform onstage, but could never work up the courage. He imagined this year wouldn't be much different.

He already enjoyed their first day, doing the 'tourist thing,' before the convention doors opened. Afterward they checked into their hotel.

The lady at the front desk informed him, rather matter of factly, that there were no more rooms available. He considered that one of the more trivial matters though. He had enough money stuffed in his wallet to get by for the next two days on his own. Not to mention the one really cute brunette in the group told him he could sleep on the floor in her room.

He promised to be a perfect gentleman in the hall outside her room, but she waved him off. She assured him she was fine with the arrangement.

His skin prickled with goose bumps as a draft of cold air rushed across his exposed feet. In his half-awake stupor, it took him a moment to notice the source of his mystery alarm clock.

Sitting open on the nearby mattress was a laptop. The victory fanfare from *Final Fantasy*, one of his favorite Japanese video games, rattled out repetitiously from its speakers.

He rose to his knees, laying his chest on the side of the bed as he hunched over the screen. Before he could even figure out what the screensaver was, he ran his finger over the touchpad, causing the noise to disappear, and the last viewed website to pop onscreen.

He lay back down, rubbing his forehead with the palm of his hand. A shiver shot down his spine as a gust of wind again rolled over his exposed feet.

They were up pretty high, he thought, remembering vaguely someone said they were on the seventh or eighth floor. It took him a moment to realize the window was open.

He staggered to his feet, adjusting his shirt and rubbing the sleep from his eyes. He blinked to orient them to the light of the city pouring in through the open window.

He crossed the room, dragging his hand along the dresser to keep himself upright.

His amber eyes reflected the gleam of the streetlights below. The dim luminance casting a shadow of his toned physique against the door to the hall. Only then did he finally think of her. He assumed she must have been hot and had opened the window, but he thought this was ridiculous! It was mid-autumn, and too cold to be leaving windows thrown wide.

He craned his head to the side, bringing a hand up to massage the stiffness from his neck. He then looked to see if she was as cold as he was.

"That's odd," he mumbled to himself when he saw the bed was empty.

He looked back to face the bathroom. The door was open, and the lights were off. Confused, his gaze again fell over the unmade bed, as he squinted to read the clock on the nightstand. He found it difficult without his contacts in.

He turned to the window, approaching it. A feeling of nausea welled in his gut as he peered down at the street below. He stood there for a moment, his vision tunneling while his head bobbed downward. Another blast of cold air brought him back, and he reached to close the window.

His hand stopped short when he heard a faint sound coming from outside. It faded into the general hum of the city for a moment, difficult to make out amidst the sounds of passing cars and the heavy wind. When he heard it again, it was muffled by the noise of distant siren.

He paused for a moment, weighing the possibilities.

Slowly, he knelt against the windowsill. His stomach felt as if it had rolled up into his chest when he began to peek his head out. His hands were slick against the frame, which he clutched tightly.

The wind rushed by, causing his hair to dance about the nape of his neck. He tried not to look down, craning his head to the left when he again heard the sound.

There she stood, on a ledge barely as wide as her feet were long, unaware of his arrival. Her face appeared vacant, as if she were miles away. A single tear traced its way down her cheek, making her emerald eyes glitter with a soft, iridescent shine as she sobbed once more.

"S-stop," he said, making sure to raise his voice enough for her to hear him.

Her head jerked towards him, and she pressed her back up hard against the wall. He had broken her concentration.

He thought he could hear her heart pounding in her chest, but it was his own, suddenly frantic.

"Please… stop." His mind raced through all of the speeches he used to give friends, trying to talk them down from break-ups or fights with their parents.

"D-don't come out here!" she shrieked, shuffling a careful step away from him.

His soft voice came again, sounding sincere, "Don't worry," he forced a chuckle. "I'm petrified of heights, remember? If I came out there, you'd be needing to save me."

"Y-you won't come any further?" she asked. He was convinced she would jump if he did.

"Hey, we rode up into the Arch together just this morning, in those tiny, little pods, swaying back and forth. You're the one who told me you could see the whites all around my eyes," he said, his voice a little shaky. The event still felt all too recent for him. He tried to forget the rattling sounds those things made on their ascent; he kept waiting for them to snap off their tracks. "Do you really think I'm going to come out there now?"

She shook her head. "You promise?"

"I swear it." He said, with a cold concreteness. "While you're just standing around... would you be interested in talking?"

It was hard to play it cool. He wanted to yell at her, and tell her to get back inside. He wanted to make this easy, to beg her, to do anything but this. He hoped reverse-psychology worked like it did in the movies.

When she didn't say anything, he felt a slight relief, hoping he had convinced her to stay and listen for a moment.

"Maybe if you told me why you want to do this, it'd make sense to me," He bade her. "It'll bother me if you don't."

Her eyes flicked onto him for a moment, but then back to the streets below. He tensed, waiting for her to do something, but she stayed there, very still.

"It'll bother you?" she smirked, a hint of sarcasm in her tone. "I wonder how it will make my parents feel..."

"I..."

"I know what you think, you think I'm just some angsty teen out here for attention, and I'm going to make a mistake I'll regret."

"Not necessarily."

"What's that supposed to mean?"

"It means: I don't know why you want to do this, but I'd like to."

"What do you want to hear? A story about my drunk of a mother? Or how about my abusive father? There are much better stories than mine."

"But I want to hear it," he glanced downward. He promised himself he wouldn't be doing *that* again.

"What can you do?" she asked, "Can you change anything?"

"I can listen."

She hung on that a moment. With a sigh, she continued.

"I was so happy to come here, to fit in. Do you know what it's like to get more love from strangers than your own family?"

"No, I can't say that I do," He answered. "I've never really liked meeting new people. I like being alone sometimes, it's peaceful."

He wondered if he had gone too far, trying to shift the topic of the conversation from the matter at hand. She gave few outwards signs to form an opinion either way.

He really wanted to ask her, 'Why me?'

He wanted to know why she had invited him to stay in her room if she was already planning this. He realized that was selfish. He couldn't be sure she had planned this.

"My grades," she started. "They... I have to move back home, I'm going to lose my scholarship, and I don't have enough money to pay for school without it. I thought I was finally free for the first time in my life... guess I was wrong."

"You don't have to if you don't want to."

"I'm only nineteen... I don't have any way to pay for school on my own, not that, and pay to live on campus."

"Nothing's impossible. There's always student loans, and—"

"Loans I'll be paying off until the end of time? Would you rather I jump off a ledge two years from now, when I get the first bill in the mail?"

"Yeah, but, there's still more than just loans even…"

"How?" she scoffed.

"Move in with friends? I'm sure—"

"I'm not going to become a burden; my friends have enough problems without me throwing my shit on them."

He sighed, deciding to abandon that road, at least for a moment. The uncomfortable silence that followed almost seemed to scream out the question he thought was on her mind: *So, are you done now? I don't have all day.*

"Ok… ok, instead of asking your reasons to die, why don't I tell you some reasons to live for?"

"You don't know me, you don't know—"

"Universal reasons," he interrupted.

"Ok, fine." She crossed her arms over her chest. He wondered if it was because she was cold, or agitated, or both.

She waited.

He turned his head towards the distance, looking for the red orb in the eastern horizon. When he spoke, it was distant, almost mysterious. He hoped she could not figure out it was faked to make his point more dramatic. "The sunrise."

"The sunrise?" she almost laughed.

"Every time I see it… It's one of the most beautiful things there is." He paused. "If that isn't a reason to wake up every day, then I don't know what is."

She huffed, "For the sun? Wake up for the fucking sun? Are you listening to yourself?"

"Are you?" he shot back. "It's hard to decide that death is the only way out, at least for me it is, but it's easy to find something worth living for, even if you have to give it importance yourself."

"You seem to know a lot about this," she countered sarcastically. "Think about killing yourself often?"

"I have," he muttered. "Not often, but I have. I think we all do at some point."

"Would you?"

"Yeah… if a horde of zombies are crawling towards me, and I've got one bullet… Bang. The End."

"I'm serious!" she sobbed.

"So am I. It's about the only thing I think that's bad enough to give up on life for."

"Zombies?"

"Yeah." He gave a sharp nod.

She sighed. A smile seemed like it wanted to curl onto her lips. He imagined it must have been some sort of irony for her, to room with one of the biggest nerds in their group—that a serious, life or death conversation could be rationalized out with… zombies.

"Fast zombies or slow ones?" She asked.

He couldn't tell if it was because she liked him, or because she was glad he would be the last person she would talk to.

"Slow ones, fuck… if there is a god, or some omnipotent being out there malicious enough to make zombies into Olympic runners, I'd shoot myself before I even got to that mall."

She laughed then, for the first time, laying all of her weight against the wall, "Which mall?"

"Any mall… there's always a mall, or some place with lots of entrances and exits. Doors made entirely of glass, or an obscene amount of windows. Plenty of places for zombies to pop out of, scare the audience, and have their brains blown out."

She started to smile. "You know, you remind me of someone I used to know."

"I take it he was incredibly handsome and very masculine?"

She laughed again, then offered him nothing more than silence.

His mouth curled back in a half grin, his nose felt numb as the wind bit his face. "Could we talk about this inside? You've got to be colder than I am, even with that jacket."

"What makes you think I'm not going to jump?" She turned her head and looked him straight in the eyes.

He blinked. Suddenly he found it difficult to match her gaze. "If you were going to, I assumed you would have already."

"I still don't have a way out of this..." she said.

"Yes you do," he said, his tone more serious than it had been for a while. He met her gaze and stared directly into those beautiful, emerald eyes. "There's always a way, if you have the will to find it."

"Name one."

"Me."

"You?"

"Yeah, you could live with me."

"You're—we're not—"

"You didn't act like you thought I was going to try anything when you invited me to sleep in your room," he explained. It made perfect sense to him. "So why would you mind sharing an apartment or something?"

"I—"

*       *       *

She could not deny his logic. She found herself unable to look away from him. His eyes lit up, a gleam caused by the earliest rays of dawn.

He leaned back, his shoulders lining up with the wall instead of reaching out beyond it. "Come on, come back in. If you change your mind, you can run back out there. You're probably faster than me anyway."

She took a step towards him.

"I'm not going back to sleep now, we'll talk about this as long as you want."

Deep down she couldn't let herself feel as though anything had changed. As much as she wanted to believe in him, it was hard for her to trust anyone. The list of people who let her down had grown steadily over the years. Something about the thought of really jumping, of really dying on that pavement below, pushed her to hope for the best this time.

She took another step towards him.

He was right. She was nineteen now. If she wanted to, she would never have to see her parents again. The thought of being completely self-sufficient scared her. It was not until then she realized how much she had depended on the money her mother sent her. If she kept both her jobs though, and he helped with the living expenses, it could almost bring things back into balance. Without her parent's help.

Another step.

She didn't know him that well, but they went to many of the same social functions, and a few of his classes were in the same building as hers. If she waited for him after class, they could ride together and save on gas money. In a few years, she would graduate, and he would be done, then who knows what could happen. She could be in control of her life for the first time.

On the last step, she slipped.

In a flash, it all went away. As she started to fall, she reached out to grab the ledge, but missed by an inch. All those visions, all those hopes and all those dreams she had mustered, of how her life could be… of how it should be. She knew none of it would ever happen.

*     *     *

He lunged out, grabbing her by the wrist.

She dangled helplessly in midair, only his straining muscles to keep her from the pavement several stories beneath her. He was almost completely out the window now, his right leg on the ledge as he used his left knee to try to secure him to the room. She scrambled to grab the ledge with her other hand, trying to support some of her weight.

All of his fear disappeared in an adrenaline surged heartbeat. He couldn't let her die now. Not when he had convinced her to come in. He couldn't let it happen.

"Not now."

He grunted, ignoring the pain coursing through his arm and into his shoulder. The sudden jerk as he stopped her fall must have pulled something out of alignment, but he ignored it and shifted his balance backwards.

It was too soon. She lost her grip on the ledge, forcing all of the weight back on him.

He readjusted, giving an inch before going back to pulling her up, slowly this time. The world around him seemed to fade into the background as he focused only on her.

"Grab my wrist tight!" he called out.

After so many tense minutes spent praying he could talk her out of jumping, he couldn't handle the idea of watching her fall by accident.

The rising sun shone through the nearby buildings now, painting over them in a soft haze of gold.

He let out a shout of exhaustion. With one final tug, he toppled over backwards, pulling her into the room and onto his chest as his back hit the floor hard.

They both heaved for a moment in silence, their chests finding a rhythm as his strength faded. He took in a deep breath.

"Y… you said you wouldn't risk coming any further," she managed, looking up at him.

"I lied."

Their heads both jerked towards the laptop on the bed as its speakers again blared out the victory fanfare from *Final Fantasy*, offering its own ironic commentary.

She started to laugh then. On the floor, laying awkwardly on top of each other, they both began to laugh in earnest.

In seconds, the room was filled with the light of the rising sun, its brilliance framed by the distant Gateway Arch.

# A Night on the Train with Trolls

By Den Dotson

Old Dan's smelled of rust and petroleum. Erik sat in a porch chair normally reserved for drinking beer in the evening and took a break to pet Ragnarok, the old junkyard dog. Erik liked Rags and Rags liked anyone who would tirelessly pet him while on the porch.

For Erik, it was more than a passing friendship with an old dog. It was in Erik's nature to love creatures that needed to be cared for and protected. Rags had been the first such creature for Erik when they were both pups. Rags had grown old and Eric had grown into early adulthood.

"We need to go," Erik said to no one in particular.

"We're going, just two more minutes," Bill replied from inside a pile of nasty looking debris. Bill was looking for *the* piece, that particular piece of junk Bill had to find before leaving. He would know it only when his eyes beheld it. Of course, it didn't matter that Bill had already found a hundred pieces he couldn't live without. No one would be leaving until he found *the* piece.

"We need to go," Erik repeated.

"Almost... got it," Bill said between metallic bangs and crashes. "Go see if Old Dan has any beer in the fridge. Bring him one and he'll go easy on me when it's time to pay."

Old Dan was never easy when it was time to pay.

The old sign over the old house, which served as Old Dan's office and living quarters, read "Old Dan's Antiques, Oddities and Metal Works". It was a junkyard. Old Dan had more junk than any place within a thousand miles. The pieces ranged from the smallest wristwatch to, at the largest, some piece of a bomber plane and several railroad cars. The oddities, as Dan liked to call them, filled every inch of space over a couple square miles from the front yard of his house off into the distance behind. To the general public, Old Dan was a source for hard to find car parts and a supplier of fixtures and such for renovating old houses. Erik, Bill and their families were some of the few people who had the run of the place. It was a look at some of Old Dan's oddities as a child that convinced young Erik his nightmares were more than just imaginary scares. Old Dan also reassured Erik as a youngster, the monster under his bed may in fact be a monster.

As Erik finished petting Rags and headed into the house to try and soften the price tag, Old Dan rounded the side of the house and stepped onto the porch.

"You boys buying or are you just here to get in the way?" Old Dan asked in a voice full of gravel. Old Dan set down a bucket full of an oily substance that occasionally splashed on it own. Erik thought he saw a fin and a flash of teeth but he couldn't be sure.

Erik turned from the house and crossed the porch to see Old Dan. Erik used his mental picture of Old Dan to measure if other people were old. Most folks seemed quite young next to Old Dan. Erik's and Bill's fathers had come out to this junkyard when they were young and Old Dan was, well, Old Dan. Erik was sure his grandfather had come out here and Old Dan was still Old Dan then too.

Old Dan would stand about six foot seven, if he ever stood upright, which he didn't. In fact, he hunched over to about five foot five, probably increasing the appearance of age. As a kid, Erik was sure Old Dan bent over to keep from blocking out the sun. The old man filled every room he walked into; he made every space feel crowded with him in it. Not to say Old Dan was fat; not one inch of him could be considered flabby. The sun had baked Old Dan to a hard crust and kept him perpetually tanned. His face creased with deep furrows and seemed to crack in new places as his face changed expressions. You would think Old Dan's ever-present wide brimmed hat would help, but the shade was too little too late. Old Dan wore his hair long in a single braid running down his back, the grey of his head and beard giving way here and there to strands of stubborn blond remaining from a day no one remembered, a day when Old Dan was just Dan.

The feature that stood out above them all was his one eye. Old Dan had worn a patch over his right eye as long as Erik or his father could remember. When he was young, all Erik wanted to do was sneak in on a sleeping Old Dan and peek under the eye patch. Could there be an eye there? An empty socket? What young boy would not want a look at that?

Old Dan pulled a dirty rag from one of the back pockets of his overalls and began to wipe his hands. The rag and the hands seemed just as dirty after the use as before.

"Bill is going to be a while," Old Dan stated as fact.

"But we need to go," Erik argued.

"Come help me out back. He will be done when we are done, you'll be going in plenty of time."

"Be done and have that stuff ready to go when I get back," Erik said to Bill, who wasn't listening.

Old Dan picked up his bucket and headed back behind the house to the wide expanse of the junkyard. To a casual observer, the area contained busted up machinery and bits of lives discarded.

Erik saw camouflage for their family heritage.

"Anyone ever see anything they are not supposed to?" Erik asked the back of Old Dan as they walked.

"Hmpf," Old Dan answered. "Like what?"

Erik approached a refrigerator once a lovely shade of avocado green now rusted to appear more like a hollowed out tree. "Like these." Erik said whipping open the door of the fridge. The air filled with fairies, iridescent and multi-colored, flittering in the fading sunlight.

"They would convince themselves they saw butterflies," Old Dan explained. "They don't want to see."

Erik knew it was the family business to keep it that way. No one should see anything, if they did he and his family would make it go away.

Old Dan walked up to a pile of cars smashed together so tight they formed a wall. The pile was so high and wide that Erik couldn't see above or around it. Inside, Old Dan kept his keepsakes from their adventures.

Old Dan opened a large truck door and stepped inside. The wall of cars was actually hollow and dark inside. Erik waited outside a moment as Old Dan flipped a switch and mercury vapor lighting flickered to life. Erik stepped into the opening and closed the "real" world behind him.

The first impression he always received in the enclosure was the smell. Hay mixed with a hint of ammonia from excrement. Then the really strange smells hit your nose. These creatures had unique dietary requirements and all of it stank.

Erik walked along and ran a hand along the cages. The kennel for exotic animals contained different sized holding pens for different sized creatures. The smallest held a fairy while it recuperated from an ailment or injury. The largest held a medium sized dragon sleeping soundly on a pile of treasure. The place was not meant to house these creatures forever. It was a halfway house where these fairy tale monsters could be cared for until safe homes could be found for them. These creatures needed to be hidden from prying eyes until they could be fed, healed, and reintroduced into the world.

"Legends have always called us killers," Old Dan began a familiar speech. "We are…"

"Caretakers of magic and wonder," Erik continued. "The last hope for enchantment to live in this world."

"I am glad to hear you have been listening," Old Dan said as he checked every latch he passed and looked in on every one of his charges. "Too many of your generation have become murderers. It's easier to destroy than to protect. We are game wardens not hunters."

"Kill only when you have failed," Erik continued the lesson, "and never fail. You and my father have taught me well All-father. I remember."

"Never forget," Old Dan turned to face him, "there will be times when you will want to, those are the times to remember."

Erik reached a hand into a cage and stroked the fur and feathers of a griffin. The half lion, half eagle glanced back at him, sensed no threat, and went back to rending some creature limb from limb and feeding the pieces to its young.

"We are running out of places to hide our finds," Erik remarked. "People are spreading everywhere. These cages should be empty."

"You don't have to teach me, boy," Old Dan growled. "I am the teacher. I know how things are going." Old Dan's voice had started out angry but ended in sadness.

Where do you hide a dragon, even a medium sized one, where some amateur spelunkers wouldn't startle it and get eaten?

Old Dan reached down and opened a feeding gate on the front of a cage. This particular occupant liked the dark and so all of the sides were covered with heavy fabric. Erik heard hissing and skin sliding across gravel as Old Dan slid the bucket through the gate. As he closed the gate, the bucket banged against the bars, and a soft munching sound followed.

"Hungry today aren't we boy?" Old Dan asked. He chuckled as he wiped his hands on his overalls. "Hard thing about that one is I keep running out of buckets. He likes to eat them after they are empty."

"I believe I heard your friend suggest you bribe me with beer," Old Dan reminded Erik. "You know until I teach Rags to be useful around here and bring 'em, someone has to go to the fridge for 'em. I have a cage to clean before you bring me another tenant. I will meet you back out front of the house."

"Sure, sure," Erik said, turning and proceeding back to the house.

*     *     *

Inside, the house was dim and musty. The office was Old Dan's territory and looked as old and oily as he did. Piles of papers with odds and ends of junk to hold them down filled the room leading up to a large oak desk and a huge office throne behind it.

Beyond the office was another matter entirely. Old Dan's wife ruled that territory. Frigg was the perfect stereotype of a sweet-as-fresh-baked-cookies grandma. Her house was frilly and spotless from the welcome mat at every door, to the kitchen where something was always cooking.

Erik wiped his feet on the mat at the door from the office and crossed through the dining room into the kitchen. Frigg was leaning over a bowl and choosing ingredients to add from bottles, tins and boxes spread around her on the table.

"Erik, child, you look hot, let me get you some lemonade," Frigg offered, heading around the table and ducking into the fridge before he could answer.

"Old Dan wanted me to bring him a beer," Erik said, "Bill and I really need to pay and go."

"You don't work here, dear," Frigg replied. "Here, have a cookie with your lemonade. Bill will certainly be a moment longer and the old man should have enough beer in his system already to hold him for a few more minutes."

Erik sat at her table and took the offered glass of lemonade. It seemed funny to Erik as he realized it never mattered what time of day or day of the week you visited Frigg, there was always food available and offered. Offered was probably too soft a word for the way Frigg served food. She brought out food and expected someone to eat it. Frigg brought over a stuffed cookie jar, removed its lid, and set it next to Erik.

"How are your folks?" Frigg asked, returning to the concoction she was mixing in the bowl. Erik recognized none of the ingredients by smell or sight.'One item resembled a wing before Frigg crumbled it and let the dust fall into her bowl.

"They are good," Erik said, "Dad worries now that I am in the family business and mom, well she is mom."

"You remind your dad how he was when he started out," Frigg said, measuring a brown powder in her hands. Erik had never seen a measuring device or a cookbook anywhere in Frigg's kitchen. The recipes flew through her mind, the measuring was all done by finger and hand, then into the oven and out with magic.

"Your father took years before he could even go out on his own," Frigg continued. "Your grandfather used to sit on that porch out there and moan to Old Dan over beer about the family tradition ending with his son. 'The legacy is over' he would wail. He would work until he died and then the world would be without.

"You men can be such babies."

"My dad took grandpa out on jobs with him for years?" Erik asked with a smile. "Years?"

"Oh, yes and occasionally after that," Frigg said, with a soft chuckle, "he was a mess. Then one afternoon, he just seemed to finally get it. He shoved aside any assistance, packed his gear and went out into the field alone. It had been the same ever since, until he trained you of course."

"Well, I do take Bill sometimes, not that he is all that much help," Erik admitted. "In fact, he is going to be going to work with me this evening if he does not hurry up. I had better take that beer now and see how it is going."

"Alright dear. You remind your folks they still know where Old Dan and Frigg live. We'll set a spot for them at the table anytime they are hungry," Frigg said with a wink.

"I will Frigg. See you soon." Erik leaned in and kissed the old woman on the cheek as he dipped into the fridge and snagged the beer.

Back out in the yard, Erik found Old Dan staring at a pile of metal and plastic Bill had gathered.

"Old Dan needs to make a living, you thieving little bastard," Old Dan said to Bill without looking up.

"Come on, Old Dan. I'm still in school, you're taking the food right out of my mouth," Bill countered.

"And knowing you ungrateful brats, you'll be back tomorrow expecting my poor old wife to give you the food too," Old Dan replied.

"Ok, we do not have time for this drama to play out," Erik jumped in. "How much does he want?"

"Two hundred," Bill said softly.

"How much do you really want?" Erik asked Old Dan.

Old Dan put on his best *"who me?"* face and then said, "One oh five."

"Pay the man," Erik said, "We are going to work."

"We?" whined Bill. "Oh no, not me. You've got plenty of time to drop me off before..." Bill looked at his watch and trailed with an "oh shit."

"'Oh shit'" is right," Erik said, "pay Old Dan while I start loading this crap in my car." Erik drove a metallic orange Ford Escape with the license plate SLA-YER on it. The small SUV was sporty enough to attract the ladies and rugged enough to haul Bill's junk around. There was even room left over for Erik's work gear and an occasional passenger.

The "oddities" Bill had so diligently sought had nothing to do with each other except in Bill's mind. Old shoes, car parts, radio tubes, tools, pipes and plenty of things Erik couldn't even identify. He just threw the stuff into the back of the vehicle and moved his backpack to the side so he could retrieve it for work.

Bill was a sculpture student at Webster University and turned the junk from Old Dan's into art. The truth was, Bill had talent. Erik could never imagine the piles they hauled over on an almost weekly basis ever finding a new life as something beautiful. Bill could imagine it, and he made it happen time and again.

There were days when he envied Bill. Erik's talents were the ones passed down to him through his ancestral line. His two brothers and one sister were not so lucky or cursed. So it fell to Erik, and after some training and some practice, he accepted his place in the world. Bill would be able to find his as well.

"Are you sure we can't swing me home?" Bill asked as he got into the car next to Erik.

"Not a chance," Erik said, waving to Old Dan and gunning the engine out of the yard. "The later it gets the harder it will get. Besides, I might need a hand on this one. And, you owe me for Hildi."

"Owe you?" Bill asked. "She so wanted me, not you."

"She did not notice either of us until I got her talking. She only noticed you because I kept talking about you. Finally, she said, 'this friend of yours sounds interesting, you should bring him around sometime.' That is when I pointed out, you sitting right next to me ogling her," Erik said.

"I do not ogle," Bill huffed, crossing his chest with his arms. Then after a moment, "She is beautiful, isn't she?"

"If you go for those tall, buxom, blonde types."

"You know you should get yourself a girl," Bill offered.

"I could have had Hildi!" Erik reminded him. Erik waited for his comment to sink in, and then relieved the tension with, "Nah, she is your type. I will know mine when I see her. Enough of the girl talk, minds on the job. We need focus. I feel something about this one."

"What is it? Your dad tell you or is it a reconnaissance mission?" Bill said, his previous mood forgotten and his curiosity fully in control.

"Trolls," Erik said, "the Eads Bridge has trolls."

"Oh god, trolls? The one night I take too long at Old Dan's and it'd have to be trolls. They stink, they slobber, they're carnivorous," Bill needlessly reminded Erik.

"If you have any change in your pocket, empty it into the console," Erik ordered. "No use getting them excited."

"Wait a minute, the Eads Bridge, they're on the train, aren't they? I hate the train," Bill moaned. "The only thing worse than trolls are the people who ride the Metrolink trains."

"The people are fine," Erik said, "and if not for me, your ass would be on that train most of the time."

"Those trains smell funny," Bill, said re-crossing his arms, uncrossing them and re-re-crossing them.

"And tonight they will smell like trolls," Erik said.

Erik pulled the car up onto the highway and left Old Dan's property behind. The junkyard was about twenty minutes from downtown St. Louis, on the Illinois side of the river, and Erik was sure it was still closer than the people of St. Louis would like it.

The young men spent much of the ride in silence, watching the sun go down behind the cityscape in the distance. As they approached the river, the city was at first next to them, and then loomed in front of them.

The sunlight glinted off the glass and steel of the downtown buildings, and the lights began to come on, as they grew close.

They crossed the river on the Poplar Street Bridge. The name was somewhat a joke, considering a highway and not Poplar Street had crossed the river for quite some time. The exit into downtown and over to the Landing was to the right.

In the distant past, Laclede's Landing was a stop for river-men working the Mississippi. Now, the Landing represented restaurants, nightclubs, casinos and bars for college kids and office workers. The area was still paved with cobblestone and lit by ornate streetlights. Erik's thick tires buzzed as they crossed the stones originally designed for horseshoes.

"It sucks we have to pay to park so we can ride the train," Bill remarked. "Do you get reimbursed for these expenses?"

"Reimbursed by who? My dad? He has trouble paying for a cup of coffee. You think we are getting rich doing this? This business should be considered charity work," Erik returned with a sigh.

Erik still tried to think of what he did as a business. Actually, it was a service, one which no one knew or could know about. About a thousand years ago, the world began to change. Mankind left behind the Dark Ages, established religions, and then turned to science to find answers. The old gods with their mystical practices and reliance on magic, who had barely held on until now, began to fade. Unfortunately, the gods were immortal, and they couldn't just stop being immortal, so they had to blend in. The stuff of legend became just that, legend. Stories were told as fairy tales to scare children or studied in schools as quaint superstitions and myths. Stories believed by simpler folks in simpler unenlightened times.

Erik, his family, and a select few knew the truth. Trolls, witches, goblins, dragons, fairies and all the old gods still very much existed. For the most part, they held down jobs when they could and caused trouble when they couldn't. The troublemakers became Erik's family's problem. He and his relatives all over the world were the last of the Knight Protectors. Their calling had been passed down through countless generations. In each family, there was one born with the talent. To Erik's parents, he was the gift. If Erik had not been born and recognized for his abilities, his parents would have gone on having children until one was born.

Erik's family received a small stipend for each incident they prevented or otherwise took care of. One advantage the old gods had found to being immortal in a mortal world was compound interest. Each of the old gods made deposits into bank accounts that were fed into secret trust funds, which funded secret foundations. The foundations paid Erik's bills and provided for his equipment. He would never be rich. He would never be famous. He would always be needed, however, and through the miracle of modern banking, he would always be provided for. Bill had asked once why the gods didn't just keep their money and live like rock stars. Old Dan had explained it was hard enough concealing their immortality; it would be impossible if any of them became a celebrity.

Erik found a reasonably inexpensive parking spot a few blocks from the edge of the Eads Bridge. The two rounded the car to the back hatch and divvied up the equipment. Each slung a backpack over a shoulder and headed for the imposing stone structure of the bridge.

Half way to their destination, Erik's cell phone rang. The ring tone was the *Flight of the Valkyries*, one of Erik's personal favorites. One of his fondest memories of childhood was a vacation his family had taken to Norway. It was among the fjords at night where Erik saw his first valkyrie in flight. It was only years later he learned the valkyrie's flight signaled the death of a warrior. He would never forget them, and it was memories like that night which kept him protecting the secrets of the old ways.

"Hello," Erik answered, breathing a little heavy under the weight he was carrying and the pace they were trying to keep.

"Are you there yet, boy?" came back Erik's father's voice. "You know they get more rowdy at night? Do you remember nothing about trolls? Hmm, tell me what you know about trolls before you go in there."

"It is for you," Erik said, tossing the phone to Bill.

"Oh, who is it?" Bill said putting the phone to his ear, "Oh, hello Mister Aegir, how are you? Trolls, oh sure I remember trolls. All right. They slobber; they stink; they infest bridges and want payment to let travelers cross, and well of course it goes without saying that they eat anyone who refuses to pay.

"…Erik, well, he seems ready as always. You know Erik. All gung-ho, take-one-for-the-team, Erik. He'd go in there and take on a troll army in his underwear if you told him he shouldn't. Or as he would say 'should not'. You could have taught him to use an occasional contraction you know. He talks like a science teacher."

"Give me that," Erik said, taking back the phone. "Dad listen, we are fine. I will call you once we are done."

"Son, are you just getting there?" Erik's dad asked.

"Yes, Bill wanted something out at Old Dan's. That is why I brought him with me," Erik explained.

"You brought Old Dan out on a troll hunt? Are you crazy, boy? Old Dan is way too important to take a chance on some troll eating him." As always Erik's father didn't listen and worried too much.

"No Dad, I brought Bill with me," Erik re-explained, "Old Dan is probably sitting down to a nice meal with Frigg about now. They really miss you, you know. They wonder why you and mom do not drive out there more."

"We will son, we will. Now, you left your money in the car, right?" Erik's dad asked.

"Did you really take grandpa out on your hunts for years?" Erik asked.

"Now, well, those were dangerous days, and don't you believe everything that crazy old woman tells you now," Erik's dad returned. "Be thorough, but be safe son. You are a hundred, make that a thousand times better than I ever was, but I am your father and I will always worry."

"I know, Dad," Erik said, "We are at the station. It is time to go to work. I will call you after."

"I am proud of you son," Erik's dad always seemed to choke up when he was really worried.

"For the gods' sake Dad, they are just trolls. Bill could do this one. Kiss mom for me and I will see you Sunday for dinner." Eric hung up, tucked away the phone and pulled the backpack up higher on his shoulder.

"You're not sending me in there alone," Bill said with a pout.

"Not a chance," Erik smiled as he said, "trolls are too much fun for you to have them all to yourself."

Erik had a special place in his heart for trolls and their kind. He was about fifteen the first time his father took him out on a "hunt". The assignment was more of reconnaissance rather than any kind of confrontation.

The Chain of Rocks Bridge in North St. Louis County had a new family of trolls living there and Erik and his father were sent to make sure they had settled into the old abandoned bridge and not onto the new active one.

Erik's father had packed a cooler full of fresh meat to feed them if they looked hungry and brought along his equipment in case there was any trouble.

"They're not evil, you know," Erik's father said in a soft voice as they walked out onto the abandoned bridge. "These creatures are our responsibility. We are above all else their caretakers."

"Then why do you carry weapons and traps?" Erik asked. "I am thinking a two handed broad sword is not what the folks down at the Zoo use to care for the animals in their care."

"Hardly," Erik's father replied. "The creatures we are managing are far more fierce than anything safely kept in a public zoo. These creatures are dangerous and destructive when not properly respected. Never forget, the weapons are our last resort. If we do our job right, no one gets hurt and these creatures are allowed to live in peace and secrecy."

Erik forced his mind back to the present as they neared the bridge. The Metrolink station for the St. Louis end of the Eads Bridge was built into a leg of the bridge itself. The supports for the bridge were brick that seemed to flow from the cobblestones right up onto the bridge and across the river to the Illinois side.

Much of the bridge had fallen into disrepair and it was the addition of the Metrolink route running beneath it that gave the old crossing a new life.

Even the Metrolink tracks were repurposed from old tracks used by the railroad in years past.

"Aw, hell no!" Bill thought aloud as he stepped into the shadow of the massive structure. The pair could already smell the urine and spoiled food odors coming from the area around the Eads Bridge station.

The smell of human waste and sweat grew thick as they entered the stairwell and the fresh air disappeared around them. The stairs wound up through the leg of the bridge and exited out onto a standard Metrolink passenger platform.

All the benches, signs, lights and vending machines associated with a Metrolink station appeared out of place here within the stonewalls of the bridge. The interior was high with arched openings looking back out over the Landing in one direction and to the Arch in the other. In Erik's mind, it more closely resembled a battlement from an ancient fortress than a stop for an urban commuter train.

Erik removed his backpack and set it between his knees as he settled onto a bench. He dug into the bag for a moment and pulled out a book on ancient mythology and warrior cults, took one last look around, and began to read. The cool river air moved the acrid smells around the cavernous space but never quite dissipated them.

It was a typical autumn evening. It had been warm during the day and had turned cold with the approach of night. Erik could smell his own breath as he watched it travel as a mist into and out of his mouth. The odors and chemicals in the air made the taste in his mouth rancid and he felt a little sick.

Shadows moved around the station and danced across the brickwork. Erik was sure he saw movement out of the corner of his eye. It was slow, then quick when he would look away, and then slow again. He noticed a bulky shadow round the bridge support and head up into the bridge's underbelly.

Rats, Erik thought. It must be rats chasing pigeons around in the dark. The movement was too scratchy-scurry like to be their trolls.

Except for the two young men and the local wildlife, the platform sat empty. The cold lighting and cool breeze made the feeling of loneliness and exposure complete.

Erik wasn't afraid. He lived in a rough neighborhood. He was normally the guy others were afraid of, not the other way around. Erik stood tall at about six foot six inches. He had long blond hair which he pulled back in a ponytail or a braid to keep it out of his way. Tonight, he sported the braid. His beard was cut into a long Van Dyke that he kept neatly groomed. He was every bit a product of his ancestry and there was no way he could hide it.

His parents were immigrants from Norway, and he had been raised to respect the old ways and to honor his heritage. The religions, thoughts and cultures of his people were in his blood. He had no interest in other subjects and had his high school report cards to prove it. It wasn't a lack of intelligence that spawned his grades. He just couldn't get interested in what they were teaching. He loved old dusty books full of formal descriptions of magic and monsters. Learning algebra seemed pointless.

At first, his parents had forced their ambitions upon him, but at some point he had embraced them as his own. He was allowed to follow his own path as he discovered it. He discovered his path led him back to his family's way of thinking. The more Erik tried to rebel against his responsibilities, the more he realized how important it was for him to embrace them. His father was always proud and his mother always supportive as long as he did his best. They were patient, and knew if they waited long enough, Erik would do the right thing. The right thing was in his blood.

Bill sat fidgeting next to Erik. He whistled and then kicked a rock around. He looked up and around at every noise.

They made for an interesting pair. Erik was big and blonde. Bill was tall but wiry with a dark complexion. Erik's hair was long. Bill's cut close. Erik wore a beard. Bill was clean-shaven.

Two less likely friends would be hard to find. In fact, they had to find each other. Bill had been doing chalk drawings on the playground in second grade, when the class bully, some clod named Randy, came over and tracked mud across the soon-to-be masterpiece. Bill jumped up to defend his work and Randy began to pummel him senseless.

It hadn't been necessary for Erik to ever touch Randy. Erik was known by reputation and by his prowess on the sports field, even in second grade.

"Randy," Erik spoke in as deep a voice as a second grader's vocal cords could muster, and Randy knew he had picked on the wrong kid.

"Uh, hi Erik," Randy said with his fist frozen in midswing. "Just talking to Bill here about messing up the playground."

"Randy, I am thinking about messing up the playground with some blood," Erik said with a sinister smile. "Maybe you might want to help?"

Randy was gone before the word "help" had faded from the air. Erik lifted Bill to his feet, dusted him off, and helped repair the drawing the best they could by the time recess was over. That day, over chalk drawings and playground politics, a life-long friendship was formed. Bill was the bard, the poet and the artist. Erik would grow to be a hero to inspire the artistic soul. Erik was Achilles to Bill's Homer.

"What if they don't show?" Bill asked hopefully.

"We get a train ride and parking bill with no payment afterwards," Erik replied. "They will come. It took me a few minutes to smell them and hear them, but now I have them. They are watching, waiting, biding their time and wondering if we will make the first move. We have all night," Erik said without looking up from his book.

"You could have told me you were bringing a book," Bill said. "I thought we could at least visit while we wait."

Erik chuckled at Bill's use of the word 'visit' like they were old women sitting at home crocheting and sipping tea.

"Not really reading the book," Erik explained. "It is an old favorite I picked up at Old Dan's. Frigg recommended it."

"Old Dan has books?" Bill asked, wondering how he missed that during his many excursions into Old Dan's treasures.

"Shhhh, listen," Erik ordered. "If you listen, you can hear them laughing and moving around under the bridge. We definitely have trolls."

Bill sat quietly and heard nothing but city noises. He heard cars moving across cobblestones. He heard drunken people moving about on the street below after a night of partying. Bill wished to be one of those lucky drunken people. He even heard a horse drawn carriage, a favorite of the tourists, the horse's hooves clomping along the street below, and the gentle ringing of the tack. Definitely no troll sounds. However, he had learned to trust Erik. This was not their first hunt together and if all went well, it probably wouldn't be their last.

As Bill continued to strain to detect even the slightest sign of a troll, the train made its appearance. First, it was a blinding light coming down the track in their direction. Then, there was the sound of metal on metal as the wheels slowed. Finally, he heard the buzz of electricity running from the wires above the track down a wand into the engine of the machine. The train whistled softly as it pushed through the air.

The train eased itself to a stop in front of them and the pneumatic doors hissed open. The air coming from in the train had a metallic smell mixed with the unmistakable scent of humanity. By the time the train reached the Eads Bridge and was about to cross the river, the crowds that relied on the train going to and from work had reached their destinations, so the cars were barely occupied but the smell of closely pressed bodies remained.

"Have I mentioned how I hate the train?" Bill asked rhetorically.

"Have I mentioned you never shut up?" Erik offered in place of an answer.

The train was decorated primarily in blue and white with small touches of red here and there. Generally, as urban commuter trains go, the Metrolink was exceptionally clean and well maintained.

Erik took a seat across from the door where they had just entered.

"They know we are here," Erik said, knowing it would put Bill on edge.

Erik expected a long night of riding the train back and forth across the bridge, waiting for the trolls to make a move. He hoped it wouldn't come to him and Bill climbing around underneath the bridge flushing them out by morning.

Erik allowed himself a few moments to take in the surroundings. A lady sat with a bag in front of her, two rows back on the opposite side of the train. Four rows back, on their side, were two young men laughing and talking. Down the aisle, between the seats, near the back of the train car, sat a troll.

To an average passenger, he would appear to be a homeless person. His hair was long, filthy and had never been combed. He had a massive head with a large nose, small eyes and a mouth full of big crooked teeth. The bone structure of his head was oversized and thick. To hold up the humongous head was a tree trunk of a neck. The neck was short, quickly becoming broad shoulders and a massive frame. Completing the image, a round belly protruded from the middle of this unkempt physique, peeking out from beneath filthy and ragged old clothes held together by magic unknown to modern tailors.

Once the train was moving, the troll wasted no time in getting to his feet and heading down the aisle.

"Pay to ride," the smelly, gross creature demanded of the young men.

The men looked up at the creature, then returned to their conversation as if they thought they had heard something and were mistaken.

"Pay to cross bridge," the troll demanded, this time shoving the one youth into the other.

Erik had his backpack off and was unzipping it as soon as he saw the troll. He would need to be quick or this situation could turn ugly right from the start.

First out of the pack was a bloody-rare piece of meat wrapped in aluminum foil. Erik unwrapped it and flung it on the floor just in front of the troll. Bill looked over to see why Erik was responding to the troll by choosing now as an appropriate time for a lunch break.

"Hey did ya' bring enough for everybody," and then after a whiff "Gaaross," Bill said, wrinkling his nose and covering his mouth. "What the hell is that?"

"Goat carcass, on whole wheat, one of Frigg's lesser known delicacies" Erik answered. "Nothing a troll likes better than a little goat. It can usually even put them off demanding payment. However, it is an acquired taste."

The troll took the bait, taking a massive hand off the young man in front of him and sniffing the air. You would have thought the most fragrant perfume had been released into the confined space, from the look of olfactory delight on the troll's face. In fact, the smell of a rotting goat carcass was perfume to a troll. Erik was sure lady trolls must spread it behind their ears and on their wrists before a night out on the town.

"I hope you doped that thing," Bill observed.

"Vicodin and Benadryl," Erik replied. "He should be quite easy to deal with when he finishes his snack."

The colossal creature made quick work of the goat remains, completely forgetting his demands of payment from the passengers for a few moments. After eating, he stood up with a bit of a swagger and headed back to the group of young men.

"We are going to have to keep him busy for a few minutes while the medicine takes effect," Erik instructed Bill.

"Busy? How am I supposed to keep a big ol' troll busy? All they like to do is beg for money, eat disgusting animals and stink. I think he can do all of those things without any help from me," Bill replied, wiping non-existent dirt from the front of his shirt.

The troll repeated his demands and Erik was sure he heard a slight slur. Erik knew the slur was probably more wishful thinking than actual chemical effect.

Erik was afraid things were close to getting out of hand when one of the young men shoved the troll to make it go away. There was only one creature worse to deal with than an angry troll on a train, and that was a drunken Old Dan after his favorite football team, the Minnesota Vikings, had lost on TV.

The troll absorbed the shove and then reached for the teenager. Before the young man could yelp, the troll grabbed him and started dragging him across seats down the length of the train.

The troll proceeded down the aisle, forcing Erik and Bill to duck as the boy was pulled over their seat.

"He'll kill that kid, ya' know," Bill said.

"No, he is just playing with him," Erik answered with a smile as he stepped into the aisle. "Still it would be best if he took on someone more his size."

Erik followed the troll down the aisle and grabbed him by the shoulder.

"I paid, let him ride," Erik offered.

"You paid…he didn't," the troll offered as way of explanation.

"Frigg's cooking just is not worth what it used to be." Erik's charm was lost on the troll. In truth, Erik just wanted to get close so he could retake control of the situation.

"Can't we get out the morning star or brandish a sword?" Bill suggested, in no way helping the situation.

"Not this time, Bill," Erik said.

Erik tapped the troll first on the right shoulder and then on the left. Each tap was harder and harder until he was shoving against the troll on one side and then the other.

"I don't think he wants to dance," Bill observed.

The hulking creature swayed back and forth and tried to reach around his body to get at Erik.

Erik couldn't possibly take on a troll in hand-to-hand combat but he was the king of tease and dodge. Tease and dodge was how Erik survived being the youngest in his family. It was a way for him to play fight with Bill and not clobber him. Tonight it would irritate a troll just long enough for some powerful chemicals to move through one massive body.

Erik was dodging and poking the creature with great success until one move when he should have dodged instead of teased.

The troll spun and was facing Erik before either of them knew what had happened.

"Another sandwich?" Erik asked, pulling another wad wrapped in foil from his jacket pocket.

The giant stretched out his back and came to his full height. Later Bill would swear the brute stood seven feet tall. A massive hand reached out for the foil and the troll seemed unable to stop reaching. He extended his arm then his shoulder followed and then his whole body came toward Erik.

Erik leaped back out of the way just as the creature landed with a heavy thud on the metal floor.

"One troll down with little fuss," Erik said, smiling with satisfaction. His job was always to try and remove the threat and keep as low a profile as possible. Trolls eating passengers on the Metrolink tended to attract folks from the evening news. Just as likely to attract attention would be a young man swinging a battle axe on a commuter train in an attempt to subdue the self-same troll. A troll eating rotten meat might gross out a train passenger or two, but it wouldn't attract cameras and reporters.

The troll was just curling up in a ball for a long nap when the train came to a stop. They were about halfway across the bridge at the time. Though the train did occasionally make stops as part of its usual routine, Erik was sure this stop was anything but on the schedule.

"I think you made the others angry," Bill said, with more than a little fear in his voice.

"Or at least curious," Erik replied, removing a large pry bar from his pack and heading toward the doors. "Let's go out and see what they want."

"Is this really the best idea?" Bill asked, knowing Erik had made up his mind long before he reached the doors and started prying them open.

"We have their attention. They are more likely to be out in the open and I would prefer a face to face confrontation to having to crawl around and smoke them out." Erik explained as the doors swung open and he stepped out onto the tracks.

"I'll sit here and keep an eye on this one," Bill said to Erik's back. Bill removed some rope from his own backpack and began to tie the troll's hands and feet.

Erik actually felt better with Bill tucked safely in the train. He wasn't sure if this would be a negotiation or a fight and Bill wasn't really good at either. Erik carried the pry bar and pulled the backpack up onto his shoulder.

The bridge under-structure, where the train tracks were located, was a series of crisscrossed beams. The design was never intended to be an easy place to take a walk. Erik needed to keep looking both down and up quickly to be sure he was staying safe from falling and safe from any surprise attackers.

The car he had just left had been near the center of the train. It took several minutes for Erik to make his way along the side of the long vehicle to see what was preventing the train from moving forward.

The area around the train was dark except for the powerful headlights shining forward. The interior of the train provided some illumination through its tinted windows. However, that light was more distracting than anything. Even though the lights of downtown St. Louis were visible in the distance, they provided little help in finding his way.

As Erik's eyes began to adjust to the dark, the bright train lights were nearly blinding. It took several minutes for his vision to clear, and even then Erik could hardly believe what he was seeing.

Huddled transfixed in the illumination of the headlight were a large female troll and a litter of troll babies. She carried one child on her hip and the others were gathered around her, tugging on already torn and tattered clothing.

Erik approached slowly and could hear the voices of the little trolls. They each pleaded, "gimmee, gimmee," in one form or another. The poor lady troll looked lost and at her wit's end.

Erik immediately surmised the situation. The small trolls explained Erik's mistaking their movements for those of rats and pigeons. This was a displaced young family of trolls looking to set up a new home. For whatever reason, the parents and their growing brood of young ones must have been run out of their previous arrangement and had decided to settle here. This development called for assistance, not combat. The small trollings were attracted to the smell of goat on Erik's hands and clothes.

Erik wandered into the group of young trolls, eight in all. Faced with a new target for their begging, the youngsters turned on Erik. From the waist down, Erik became all arms, heads and cries of "gimmee, gimmee."

The troll mother smiled with pride, or was it joy because she could have even one moment of relative peace? Erik motioned for them to follow, then led the smelly, dirty, hyperactive family along the tracks and back to the train where he had left their dad snoozing. Erik appreciated the mother motioning her little ones to her; it would save him a night of chasing them through the framework of the bridge. Erik encouraged the trollings to stay with him by pulling small goat morsels from his backpack. He smiled as he thought how grossed out Bill would be if he knew what part of the goat these little pieces were from. He also knew the bite sized chunks were a delicacy to trolls the world over.

"Who is your daddy?" Erik said with a smile as he entered the train surrounded by troll babies. With new people to pester, the children playfully spread out within the train and accosted each and every passenger, bringing no harm. The original eight had been joined by five more who had been shy and waited in the shadows for the all clear.

"We have a troll daycare?" Bill asked. "What are we supposed to do with these?"

"I have an idea," Erik said. "Give me the phone and clear the doors. I think the train will be moving again shortly."

Right on cue, the train lurched into motion, its path cleared. Erik moved through his speed dial numbers so he could make his calls.

"Old Dan, take off your slippers and bring the trailer. We have a whole family here." Erik clicked the phone and dialed the next number.

"Dad, meet Eric and I at the East St. Louis station and hurry up." Erik turned to Bill. "Bill, look in your backpack for snacks. We need to keep this family entertained until the back-up arrives."

Bill fished out bits of old meat from past excursions. He quickly exhausted his scraps and began negotiating with the old lady on the train to sell him her groceries.

"We are going to sit at the East St. Louis station at night with a family of trolls?" Bill asked, already knowing the answer.

"Yes," Erik answered as if Bill had asked if the sun rose every morning and the sky were blue. "Would you mug a family of trolls if you saw them?"

"Well, no," Bill admitted. "But how do we keep them together? Why did they even follow you onto the train?"

"I smell of goat and their father," Erik answered. "Trolls have little beady eyes and big bulbous noses. They live and die by their sense of smell. I smelled like home and as long as I do not shower they will follow me anywhere. Now the downside is if we do not feed them soon they will probably try to eat these passengers."

"The daddy troll never ate his second sandwich," Bill offered. "Where is it?"

"Under him," Erik answered. "Let us roll him over and feed these kids."

The troll mother had already started to minister to her husband. She gnawed on his bindings and shook him to wake him. "He is ok." Erik reassured her. "Just sleepy."

"Help us roll him over," Erik asked as much with hand motions as with words.

The lady troll seemed to understand and the three of them rolled him over. Sure enough, smashed under him was the bloody aluminum foil filled with goat guts.

Before the body even rolled over, the little trolls were tearing at the foil and meat.

Erik snatched it from them and pushed his fingers into the wet flesh. He wanted to remove the hidden drugs before he gave a group of youngsters an overdose.

He hid what he was doing by tearing off bits he had inspected and handing it to the nearest outreached hand.

The lady troll sat with her husband's head in her lap, softly sang a wordless tune, and stroked his hair. Erik felt sad for this little family. A family with thirteen children seems large in human terms, but a troll mother can give birth to fifteen trollings in a single litter. These troll parents were young and just getting started. A cage back at Old Dan's wouldn't be enough. He could have held one or two trolls for a while but a family would need a home. A home would need to be a place away from the city and safe for them to build a life.

Just as the last of the goat parts were devoured and the children were growing restless, the train pulled into the station and the doors opened with an intake of night air.

Old Dan stood on the platform with a trash can full of more goat and a smile on his face. Erik smiled back. It was moments like this when Erik loved his life. He had saved a new family and no one had died.

He thought about the small things he took for granted. Old Dan should not have been able to get to the platform before the train. Yet, here he stood and behind him in the parking lot was an old beat up panel truck attached to an old beat up trailer.

Old Dan waved bloody goat meat at the trolls and they practically danced out of the train and into his arms. The little ones had been starving on the Eads Bridge. A metropolitan bridge was no place to find food. Trying to feed his family on scraps of fast food and handouts would have ended badly eventually. To feed his family, the troll dad would have started bringing home human meat for dinner.

A brood of trolls raised on human meat would be killers beyond redemption by the time they reached adolescence. Erik had gotten to them in time.

These creatures deserved a chance to live as the gods had intended.

*    *    *

It was morning as Erik's dad and Old Dan finished hosing out the large moving truck.

"I'll never get the smell out of here you know. Never. From now on this will have to be the troll trolley. No one will want their things moved in this stinking truck," Old Dan complained as they did their best to return his property to the way they had found it.

Erik and Bill watched the goats moving about the field looking for breakfast and occasionally looking over a shoulder at their new neighbors. Goats knew trolls as well as trolls knew goats. Whether they liked it or not, the goats were well aware that they had just moved to the top of the menu.

Across the field, the little troll family was moving into their new home. It wasn't much to look at, but to a troll it was a dream come true. Old Dan had found them an old covered bridge on an abandoned dirt road next to a goat farmer who owed some really big favors… for what, Erik would never know.

Old Dan had given Erik a list of numbers to call while they had driven their fully loaded rattletrap far from the city. It had taken well into the afternoon to find them an available spot. Out here in the country, the new family would have a bridge to call home where they couldn't really hurt anyone, and plenty to eat.

"You should be proud of this one," Old Dan said to Erik's father, with a hand on his shoulder, indicating a good deal of pride himself. "It is rare for a warrior to better himself in his children."

"All-Father, you are going to turn my head with such talk," Erik's father replied, using Old Dan's honorific in private.

"Now don't take all the credit, you young braggart," Old Dan said, returning to a more characteristic speech pattern that somehow never wholly managed to hide his affection. "He has good, hearty blood in his veins, you know."

"I know, All-Father. His is our achievement. It is the reason we all still watch over him," Erik's father said.

The two watched as Bill and Erik made their way over to the bridge to make sure the troll family was settling in. The young men got into an unexpected wrestling match with a couple of the little trolls and laughed as they tumbled in the grass.

"Were we ever young enough to stay up all night and still want to play with troll babies in the grass?" Erik's father asked.

"You aren't too old to come by and visit the old folks once in a while," Old Dan said. "Frigg misses you something awful. She has a soft heart for you, boy."

"I know, I know. I'll make time. I promise. Maybe now that Erik can handle most of this on his own, it's time to retire and visit with family," Erik's father said wistfully.

"Who said anything about retiring? In this family, we just pick something else and learn a new trade so we keep on going. You don't see me retiring do ya'? Damn lazy kids today." Old Dan grumbled with no real malice.

"I guess it's time for a change then. This life belongs to Erik now."

# ANCESTOR

## An Ode to Nelson Hamilton Aton

By Jane Wallace Reed

His hands of anvil fire healed equine pain,
nailed U's of iron into the proud hooves of
stallion, mare, and filly, whose blood ran Kentucky blue

Ben Franklin of farm implements and hillside plows,
a machinist whose cogs and wheels churned out
eleven children to run like the wind, wild with mountain laurel,
fat with joy, like sunflowers dotting hillside gardens
children who scuff-shoed their way into procreation,
until I came along, born in the city of the gleaming Arch,
destined to look for this grandfather's own great-greats,
lost in the annals of anonymity

I know that when I find them, I will not be able to see their smiles,
any more than I was able to touch his face, all shine on a summer high-noon,
but knew him only as the middle man, with hands of anvil fire

# Perry

By Jane Wallace Reed

Perry could still feel the beat of the music in his chest. He kicked at the soggy, empty cigarette pack, and he swiftly sent a crushed can flying in the opposite direction, into the night air. All so much garbage, like what Garvin had tried to feed him tonight. The rain began pelting down as he rounded Broadway and Olive.

Perry remembered his first practice with Garvin, the hope, the pride, and the laughter. Garvin had entered the Rooster's Paradise with that wild laugh of his, a new breath to the combo. Other members of the band might have easily marked this addition to their group as big time, full-of-himself. Perry knew better, because Perry knew people like he knew what made the Blues deep and real. Just like he knew how jazz was all electricity, the notes just controlled speed.

Without warning, more rain ripped, and slapped his body around. The blocks of downtown St. Louis seemed like they were about to be swept into the Mississippi River. He had to take refuge on Washington Avenue, in the wide marble-roofed expanse joining two office buildings. Safe from the rain, he laughed to himself. Sometimes, it felt good to make Garvin squirm a little. Just when Perry could hear Garvin's stiletto yet velvet-tinged strokes on the bass really warming up the club, Perry would crash things.

"You gotta' be up where you're down now man, too much drifting there in the middle of it, too loose - love ya' man, but - you know." Perry would call out. Cocky though Garvin was in every other detail of his life, Perry recognized his buddy's vulnerability at rehearsals.

Perry fixated on the cascading roar, the hypnotic curtain separating him from his city streets. "Great stuff - you're a genius - you deserved it," Perry had expressed, as he led the others in the applause when Garvin took top honors at a jazz festival in Chicago only three weeks before.

So, what was Garvin's problem? How could he shove stuff like "You're too outa' control, Perry" down his throat? How could Garvin tell him what was "wrong?"

"God," Perry swore. At least nobody was around to see the side-show he was putting on now, as the water leaked from his eyes. "Jesus, Jesus, Jesus - get a grip," he implored himself. "Just 'cause some hack of a buddy tells you to get help - doesn't mean you need it."

Then, he heard it. Deep in the recesses of the marble shelter, as he turned toward it, the bag in the corner moved. He would dive into the river of rain, he thought. He heard the creaking sounds of the small, bony woman as she came from under the rag-bag pile, like a sinewy-throated chick from an egg. He felt her looking at him, yet through him. A lost animal, her wailing voice pierced the darkness, "If you treat them nice, they'll let you in." She made crumpling noises, again melting into her own Oz of blankets.

He wished he could melt into the wall holding up his shaking frame. When had people decided that he should not take chances, not be allowed to be angry in his own way? He straightened his back as he realized that the rain sounds filling his ears had changed from sharp-edged ragged to soft-steady, and had made it possible to finally make it home.

Now he could step into the cool night, hopefully less populated with the usual chorus of partying voices. Voices, that on most nights, rounded every corner, invading his thoughts as he crossed the intersections. Some things about his nightly walk he welcomed, like the comforting, familiar wafts of hops that issued from the Busch brewery.

When Perry was an adolescent, this sweet, unique smell summoned up a childhood loneliness that was only explained later to him by his mother. She spoke of how, as a toddler, he had to go to a nearby downtown daycare center, just for one month. And even though she picked him up each evening, he would cry fiercely once he was in the circle of her arms.

Perry decided he would talk to Garvin Sunday night, and would let him know how he had not meant to be "all over the map."

A man running down the sidewalk, afraid of the rain turning back into torrents, rushed past Perry, almost knocking him into the street.

Perry pushed onward, into the now moderate downpour, anxious to be in his apartment, with its myriad of plants and sheets of music he could run his fingers over. His cane tapped the familiar sidewalk in front of him, acutely aware of the depth of puddles in his path. Why couldn't the world just go away and leave a blind man alone?

# The Homecoming

By Jane Wallace Reed

Earl lived in a fine house now, a real house. It was made of brick and wood, with a huge kitchen where the light poured in from fancy bay windows. The real estate agent had assured him that these were the signs of prosperity, not to mention he lived in "one of the finest St. Louis neighborhoods."

"Amenities, landscaping, patio, deck," were, to some, familiar words since birth. Earl's ears, eyes, and soul soaked them in like water to a man in the desert. Everything in St. Louis had a special warmth for Earl. He loved the beauty and charm of Forest Park with its lakes and trees, its World's Fair pavilion and waterfall, the Zoo and the inspiring panorama of its museum, perched-high-atop Art Hill.

Earl liked to drive into the city with its amazing Union Station. Once, trains had click-clacked into the iron and glass canopy, now, families gathered around its placid lake and fine restaurants. St. Louis was very much a big city with that little town feel Earl needed to give him a sense of newness, yet familiarity. Soon, he would have someone to share in all this.

It was autumn now, as Earl looked out the windows of his western suburbs home, with its hills and green surroundings, but Earl remembered when crickets swallowed up the night. He remembered the other place, of a thousand more crickets, and a thousand years ago.

"Mountain man," they used to tease him when he came to work those first days in the towns. Wild like the deer, the possums, the bears, he had flourished in the Kentucky hills.

Mama called from the porch "Earl, Earl, Earl Painter Preston, git on in here, boy." A hot meal, if he had worked himself up a good appetite, could make him show heels to a mountain cat.

Laughter was as plentiful as the mountain rains, which when they was want to come, spared 'narey a body. Sometimes as he and Mama were sprinting around, gathering up pots to catch roof leaks, she would burst right out in song "Fill them pots with water, fill 'em good and right, so we kin be out dancin' in the pale moonlight."

Mama didn't look like she'd danced in a good long time. At 5'2", she was strong, but always black under the eyes. A sun-lined face held a delicate, upturned nose, eyes that were uneven, but full and sad, and determined chin. For her age, her hair had silvered far too soon.

When the sunny days wrapped one clear around the other, and marauding mosquitoes and fly squadrons zoomed on their planned routes, with firefly replacements winking through the night, Earl felt alive. All of a sudden, on some of these sultry noon days, Mama would lay herself down for a nap. Now and again Earl would ease into the house, for a beef jerky or apple, careful not to slam the screen door, using a gentle-slow closing. Then he heard them. His Mama's familiar muffled sobs, escaped in the lumpy, yellowed pillow with its stripes and stains, covered by one of the three sets of pillowcases that Mama kept washed.

Seemed like the linens and clothes were never just still. They were waving to the rare passing neighbor as they swung from a line, or sunning themselves on rocks, or diving down washboards into lye-smelling pools.

Earl knew most rightly what the sobs felt like, 'cause they were dried and waiting, somewhere in the tightness of his own belly. Sometimes, their mutual feelings would spring up in the open. Just like the copperheads, when you crossed into their territory.

He always wanted to know his father, who abandoned him and his mother shortly after Earl was born. "What was he like, Mama? Do I look like him?"

Earl memorized what Mama said, "Jet-black hair, with wisps like fine smoke, eyes blue as that there sky... had himself a strong chin - that divided kind of deep-like in tha' middle - they got a name for it, cliff... 'cause it's so deep, you could fall right into it, I guess... strongest arms I ever seen or felt on a man. But, real pale, white skin, said it was from his Irish grandmother...' Though he couldn't hold no candle to you my hansom' baby, but if ya' decidin' to get a big head, don't bother none, I got me a big, big switch."

Mama had whipped him a total of, maybe, four times in his whole life. One was for gitten' lost deep in the big woods, 'til she was gone as mad as Ol' Miss Hammond, up the holler.

Earl's third question "Did he love me, Mama?" was always answered the same. "Does God love the earth? Does the stars come out at night? Does you know your own name?"

Earl spoke with his Papa on lots of occasions. Once, on his favorite log, seated, and brushing a wood-spider off his thigh, he told Papa that if he would come back real soon, Earl would grow up to be a storekeeper, in the valley, smack dab in the middle of Odenton. Another time he promised his Papa he would grow up to be a famous baseball player, and when people wanted him to sign baseballs, he would put Earl Painter Preston, son of Arnie Earl Preston, on every single one.

He wished he'd promised Mama instead. The wind wailed cold, and blew hard, and deep when they tossed the last shovel full of dirt onto Mama's pine box. Jimmy Anderson strummed out "Amazing Grace," Mama's all-time favorite hymn, Mrs. Wilkens supplied the plastic lilies, and Bobby-John Brinker, the corn-liquor. Somewhere between the chords of "A wretch like me," and "I once was lost," Earl then and there decided he would never talk to Papa again.

Now, as a man of mature years, standing in the front hallway of his new home, he was waiting. Gilbert Greenlow, a long-time friend, had told Earl about a special group that worked, using the latest computer programs, to find just about anybody you lost, or as in Papa's case, lost you.

Earl waited, because in fifteen minutes to one-half an hour, generous friends would bring Earl's father into this house to live out the rest of his life, with the son he had never known. Earl had taken up the search for his father only eight years ago. He had originally moved to Missouri, because his wife's family came from these parts.

Pacing back into the living room, he sat down and rested his tired back against the simple blue sofa in the new, sparsely furnished living room. How strange that the search had located Papa in the same state.

Someday, when Papa was settled in, Earl would take to explaining the details of his grown-up life. From the time of his nineteen-year-old entry into real towns, later real cities, from handy-man and shoe salesman jobs to his now excellent, long-term construction supervisor position, he changed. He had grown into the customs of the world, like red-bud trees that stood out in early spring. From rooming houses to apartments, some not so nice, some clean and spacious, he moved.

He learned love through Clarinda and Cloe and Abigail. At the age of forty, God took his wife and two little girls away, at the hands of a drunk driver. Earl would spare Papa this information for a while. Aloneness had eaten away at Earl like it used to, now and again, in the hills.

Then, only the sound of a whippoorwill, with its plaintive voice, would break the coldness of the woods, or the sharpness of a pine tree. Like most listening souls, Earl would wait for some far-off answer to its call, but it never came. No voice echoed a return reply, no sounds acknowledged the bird's reaching-out song.

"I've got lots of pictures to show him," Earl thought, moving from sofa to window, for yet another searching view of the empty driveway in front of his property. Evening hung on the edge of this autumn afternoon, when the maroon car finally drove up the suburban, blacktop road. Earl opened the door with its oval glass center, and hurried across the porch, and down, crunching the red and yellow leaves scattered along the way, over steps and driveway.

His two friends, who had insisted he wait at home, climbed out of the front seat. Gilbert, who had been driving, called to Earl, "safe and sound." He then pulled the handle of the back passenger door open, and helped the frail, old man out. He had a skinny-chicken walk, and he looked like he might be blown over by a breeze.

Earl reacted instantly. "Fathers are always bigger than you." He felt a catch in his chest at this silent voice from a dependent child's brain.

Where he had been frozen, Earl moved quickly now. "Papa, welcome, welcome - it's me, your son, Earl." His mother had been right - skin as pale as a bed sheet. With the bleaching of age, it was intensified, save for the brown splotches that are a common geriatric gift.

Vacant blue eyes, beaten eyes, took in Earl's greeting. Then, bowing the fuzzy clumped whiteness of his head, with all the politeness of a Japanese tea ceremony, he mumbled in a trembling, hesitant voice. "Hello, son. You are so good." Next spring, he'll be heavier and more alive, Earl forecast to himself.

Earl had given up hate a long, long time ago. As the friends climbed back into the car, with only mute waves to his grateful glances and thank-yous, he put a supportive arm around his father.

"Papa, they say the temperature's going to drop tonight. I thought maybe an early fire in the fireplace would be good." They stood now at the top of the steps.

The old man lifted and tipped his head in Earl's direction, "A fire, oh yes, son, I would really like that."

# Molly

By Mike Beckett

The dog comes out of nowhere. Honest. I never see it coming. Nobody does. Not me. Not my eight-year-old son Jimmy in the seat next to me. Not the driver of the Hummer behind us.

I cruise down Highway 159 with my son in a brand new midnight blue Honda.

Behind me, a canary-yellow Hummer rides my tail like an overgrown bumblebee.

It's a gray Sunday afternoon in November, and Jimmy's just lost the soccer game, 12-2, another spanking by Midwest Fury. Jimmy won't shake it off. "It's just one game," I tell him.

"I stink at soccer," he says. "I'm not playing anymore."

"Oh, yes you are. And you're going to get out there and practice more before the games, aren't you?"

No reply. The air in the car feels icy. Good.

Besides the soccer loss, today's the anniversary. Five years. I always hate this day.

Jimmy's ocean blue eyes-her eyes-look down through a curtain bang of blonde hair-her hair. His little fingers-probably hers as well-jitter on his orange and green striped athletic shorts. One white, grass-stained shin guard jiggles up and down with his leg.

Then this dog, a skinny, tan-colored dog, shoots straight for my right front tire. The dog wants me to hit it, wants me to plow right over it and crush it. I have no time to react or think about what to do.

Brake pads scream. The seatbelt tightens across my waist and chest. A wet bump and crunch. More brake pads scream behind me. The world jars. Skull hits the headrest. Glass crackles.

A Hummer has a curb weight of six thousand four hundred pounds. My Honda weighs only three thousand one hundred pounds. Three tons versus one and a half tons.

Yeah.

A Hummer rear-ending a Honda sounds like a slap of storm lightning through a fifty-year-old oak tree. Now both sounds haunt me in my dreams.

One second I try to miss a suicidal dog. The next second I try to miss the curb.

Jimmy bounces first against the passenger door, then against my right shoulder. A balloon mushrooms behind him, his side curtain air bag. A cloud of minty powder fills the cabin.

When the Hummer hits the rear bumper of the Honda, an electrical impulse ignites a gas generator tucked away in the car's frame. At three hundred degrees Celsius, sodium azide decomposes into sodium metal and nitrogen gas, just enough nitrogen to inflate a side curtain air bag like a mushroom balloon. And it smells minty.

I read Popular Mechanics.

Just that quickly, it's over. "You okay?" I ask.

Jimmy nods. "Yeah."

"Get out."

"Okay."

The driver of the Hummer is a kid in baggy jeans standing on the curb and running his hands through his bleach highlighted hair. He looks not much older than Jimmy. What kind of dad would let his kid drive the Hummer?

Police arrive, and a female cop steps out. She talks to me, but all I can think is, they really have strict physical training on the force. She looks *hot* in that uniform.

She says, "Sir, can I see your driver's license?"

I'm playing as if I'm dazed, but actually, I'm checking her out. She has severe brunette hair, tied together with sticks in the back. And dark brown lipstick. Was that regulation?

"Sir? Your license?"

*Stop checking out the cop and cooperate with her. And take care of our eight-year-old son.*

After handing over my driver's license, I glance at Jimmy. He's rubbing his elbow and staring at the stringy mess of meat and tan-colored fur underneath the cars.

"Jimmy, get over here."

My son really is dazed, complete with the thousand-yard stare of a hurricane victim.

"Boy, get over here, *now.*"

An ambulance arrives and paramedics hop out. Two emergency medical technicians sit me down on the sidewalk. They sit Jimmy down next to me, his cleats slipping on the pavement. They feel our neck, our shoulders, and Jimmy's elbow. They ask us questions and look into our eyes.

Baggy Jeans kid talks on his cell phone and waves off help.

I get my first look at the state of my new Honda. It's two-thirds shorter. The back third sags like modern art made from scrap metal.

How did we survive that?

The Hummer has a dented grill. Oh, and a smashed right front headlight.

The gruesome road kill stretches four feet from the Honda's oil pan to the forward axle of the Hummer. I can't take my eyes off it.

"Stupid dog," I say to nobody.

The EMT pauses with his hands on my neck muscles. "What?"

I look directly at the EMT. "What about the stupid dog?"

He looks at me as if I'd spoken Chinese.

When you suffer from clinical depression, you see the world through a gray filter devoid of emotion. Your soul has eaten its fill on euphoria and despair and wants to be left alone now, thank you very much. It's done.

I can hear Jimmy in his bedroom crying into the pillow, soaking it with fresh tears. This is ridiculous. It's true, he lost his mother five years ago today, but that's not why he's crying. He's crying because of the dog.

*You should go see him, honey.*

My soul remembers the numbness, that wonderful defense mechanism my emotions use as a dam against the oncoming flood. The deadness feels comfortable and familiar, like the return of a worn pair of tennis shoes. I put on those old Nike Airs again.

*Go to him.*

I sit on the couch in the living room and pour another shot of Jack Daniel's. No, you don't understand. Your post-partum depression was nothing like this. This is different, more difficult, more complicated. Besides, you left *me*.

Tooper shows up, hobbling on three legs. She hops onto my lap and gives me a bone-rattling purr. Jimmy sniffs and cries some more.

Prozac helps. So does Zoloft. I have my stash, just in case. The support group for single parents at church helps as well, as does Hank Larson, the licensed church counselor. Without him, there'd be neither Prozac nor Zoloft.

*That shot of Jack Daniel's doesn't, though.*

Yeah, well, as I said, this is different.

*But you know I wouldn't drink it away.*

Jimmy's feet shuffle across the carpet. "Dad," he says in a phlegm-filled voice. Her voice. "We killed a dog."

My son weeps tears of accusation. Rachel accused me of being cold. Is he starting in on me, too?

Slouching on the couch makes me aware of new pains in my neck, my shoulders. My chest hurts as well, a bruise from the seatbelt strap. That was a bad accident. Out the window, I see the rental sitting in the driveway, a white Ford sedan. I hate Fords.

Jimmy wipes his nose on his sleeve. "Why'd she have to die?" He sounds like he did when he found out about his mom.

"What, do you think I *wanted* to hit the dog?"

Jimmy's lower lip quivers, just like Rachel's. "No," he blubbers.

Tooper fills the living room with her purring. Her back arches in delight, sending ripples through her tabby stripes. She's hungry, oblivious that her world almost turned upside down.

Now I think about that suicidal dog, the one we hit, or the one that hit us. I know nothing about it, not its name, its gender, its owner, nothing. To me, it represents nothing but road kill. It happens all the time, right? But this road kill took my new car and almost took our lives.

Nobody thinks about the soccer game, the 12-2 spanking by Midwest Fury. Nobody thinks about what happened on this day five years ago. Heck, nobody even thinks about the accident. Just the dog, the stupid dog.

"Look, Jimmy, I don't care about the stupid dog. We were in an accident. We could have *died*. And the car's totaled-"

Jimmy's face screws up for another bout of crying.

*Stop it. You're hurting him. Just be quiet and embrace him.*

I told you, this is different. It doesn't work that way. And you stay out of this.

Jimmy raises his arms for a hug, and I have to do *something*. I finish my shot, slam it on the coffee table, and stand. "Go to your room, and sleep it off."

I stride out the door and retreat to my workshop in the garage. I just have to gather my thoughts, catch up. But then she starts in.

*Our only son who lost me at age three just undergoes another tragedy, and you're emotionally constipated?*

What, are you surprised?

*You weren't always cold, honey. Remember the day you brought Tooper home?*

It was Jimmy's second birthday. In search of a gift, I noticed a crowd at PetSmart. Volunteers from the local branch of the Illinois Humane Society were hosting Adopt-A-Pet, and I thought, *perfect!*

*You found a gray tabby kitten lacking a right front leg. She had such a sweet nature, you just couldn't resist. When you brought her home, Jimmy lit up like a firefly.*

I held the kitten up for them to see. "She's a trooper, isn't she?"

And Jimmy said, "Yeah, she a tooper."

*Remember how we giggled?*

Alright, enough. Time to go back inside and make dinner.

*       *       *

I stand at the end of my driveway at two in the morning with a trash bag and a shovel. The dream replays in my mind.

"Sweetie?"

I lie in bed, listening to our three-year-old son cough in the next room.

"Hey, Sweetie?"

The digital clock reads 3:13, and rain patters against the window. The covers feel cooler than usual. I shiver. Why are the covers so cold?

"Sweetie, Jimmy's coughing."

My wife must be in REM sleep. She was so tired, wasn't she? Usually a peep wakes her, but Jimmy's hacking up a lung and she doesn't budge.

"Did you give him his medicine?"

I give her a gentle nudge. The skin of her shoulder feels cool to the touch, firm and dry like plastic. Lightning flashes right outside the window, illuminating her blank, glassy eyes.

"Sweetie? *Rachel?*"

Thunder crashes. And my world turns upside down.

Tonight, Rachel's glassy eyes then turn to me and shine in the lightning flash. *"What about the dog?"* she whispers.

And I wake up, get dressed, rummage through the kitchen for a trash bag, and retrieve the shovel from the shed.

Five years. I always hate anniversary day.

Doctors call it an *ischemic cerebrovascular accident*, or CVA for short, but most people just call it a stroke. An embolism migrates up the carotid artery to land in the brain. It lodges itself at an arterial intersection, cutting off the blood supply to vital sections of the brain, a condition doctors label *ischemia*. The part of the brain experiencing blood loss determines the severity of the attack. During severe ischemic attacks, otherwise known as "lucky strokes," ischemia occurs in the brain stem, which handles involuntary functions. Like breathing.

Thinking about the mechanics of the process helps. It's not a person, it's not Rachel; it's a faulty machine.

Rachel had been complaining about a pain in her leg for days. Forty-two minutes after Rachel fell asleep that night, the pain broke free, traveled up a vein into the heart, traveled up the carotid artery, and stayed just close enough to the brain stem to make her body forget to breath.

The stroke is anything but lucky. And my life turns upside down.

*Why do you still think about me, honey? You have our son to raise. Just move on.*

My eyes shift compulsively to the fifty-year-old oak tree by the bedroom window, split down the middle. The pain of loss, the memory of finding Rachel, still aches. Five years and a day have passed since she departed, but I still feel it every time I see that tree. A silent voice screams inside, wanting release, wanting to be heard, but I tell it no, not this time. Not again. Never again.

With effort, I stop myself from sinking in the mire of memories and climb back to the present. My eyes are squeezed shut, and I open them to see oak leaves scurry across the driveway, blurred by angry tears.

Why do I even look at that tree? Why don't I chop it down and forget about it?

*Because you can't let go, honey.*

Now I stand at the end of my driveway with a trash bag and a shovel and a steely resolve devoid of emotion.

*　　*　　*

Since I won't have a peaceful sleep with that dog still on the road, and since Rachel won't leave me alone, I have to do *something*.

A street lamp casts a soft golden pool that covers the gravel road, the driveway, the yard. Oak leaves rustle across the gravel and bounce off my sweatpants. My left hand holds a black garbage bag, a heavy-duty lawn bag, sixty-gallon capacity, two-ply. The breeze doesn't even nudge it. My right hand holds my new shovel I bought over the summer. The black steel blade glitters in the golden street light. The yellow, forty-seven-inch fiberglass handle looks like a neon glow stick in the night.

What am I doing?

There are times in my life when sanity is not a question. The purpose of a particular action presents itself as self-evident, requiring neither excuse nor explanation. This is not one of those times. Why else would I analyze my shovel and my garbage bag?

Monday morning. My watch reads 2:05. I have to be in the office in five hours, and instead of sleeping, I'm standing by the street, holding a garbage bag and a shovel and questioning my own sanity.

What am I doing?

I'm obeying the voice of my dead wife, that's what I'm doing. Yeah, that's perfectly sane.

I glance back at the house, a 1950s ranch-style nestled between two other identical houses in a mature, established subdivision. People who live here are normal, sensible, and sane. They don't listen to their dead wives and take predawn excursions to rescue road kill. And they don't leave their eight-year-old sons alone in the house.

That gives me pause. I locked the doors and checked on Jimmy before leaving, hearing him snoring. Still, what would the neighbors think if they knew I left my son alone in the house at night?

Recollections of midnight shots of Jack Daniel's play in my mind. Jimmy always sleeps through them, snoring away, sometimes talking in his sleep, but he sleeps all the same. He might wake up and be a little scared, but he'll survive. Besides, this won't take long.

I set off down the street, exit the subdivision, and walk on the sidewalk along the highway. The breeze carries the distant noises of the interstate, with the sound of an eighteen-wheeler downshifting.

Despite the apparent madness, I do have a plan for tonight. I can't resurrect my wife, I can't restore my Honda, and I can't undo killing that stupid dog, but at least I can return the dog to its owner. If doing that will end the dreams, then it's worth it.

Pets usually have ID tags, which the Humane Society can use to find their owners. Tooper never could abide a collar; instead, she has a microchip embedded above her shoulder blades.

The cold November breeze whips through me, so I pull up my jacket collar. I should have worn my heavy leather coat. What was I thinking?

If people ever found Tooper dead somewhere, they could take her to the Humane Society and scan her microchip. That's how they'd find me.

Maybe the dog has a microchip as well. Maybe the dog even has an ID collar. Who knows?

Manufacturers call them radio frequency identification (RFID) transponders, but the good folks at the animal shelter just call them microchips. Inside a polymer casing rests a silicon chip with a small antenna array. The silicon chip stores data about the animal and its owner, and the antennae transmit this information over radio waves. It requires no internal power source; it simply stores and transmits.

That's it. Think about silicon chips. Think about technology. Think about anything but what I'm doing out here tonight.

People come across RFIDs everyday when they buy t-shirts at The Gap or CDs at Wal-Mart. By scanning the items, the cashiers turn off the microscopic transponders. No more signals to trigger the door alarms when they leave.

After I submitted the paperwork to adopt Tooper, they scanned the top of her shoulder blades with an electronic gun to store the information. They'd use the same gun to retrieve the data from the dead dog, if it has an RFID.

Finally, I arrive without anyone stopping to ask what I'm doing with a trash bag and a shovel at two in the morning. In front of me lies the dog scraped across the pavement, a furry interruption in a long, black tire track. Glass fragments surround the body, making it the gory center of a starry constellation.

This is nuts. What am I doing?

Before I think twice, I kneel down, place the open trash bag on the ground, and begin scouring the corpse off the road with my shovel. I can't get the whole thing up in one scoop. Wet things slide off the shovel and plop to the pavement. The smell of entrails makes me hold my breath.

Focus on my shovel. Concentrate on the sounds of the nearby interstate. Scoop into the bag. Look for oncoming cars. Think about the fascinating microchips. Just don't think about what you're doing right now.

Still, I can't help but notice: the dog's a female. It's a *she*. I see an ID tag as well, but scratches in the metal hide any useful information.

After an eternity of scraping and scooping, the entire dog now lies in my garbage bag.

The term *deadweight* refers to a very heavy object, difficult to carry. Sailors use the word to describe a ship's fully loaded displacement, because of whalers who used to haul dead whales behind the ship. As I walk back toward the subdivision, this word comes to mind. The dead dog feels like a sack of bricks in the trash bag.

I return to the house and hang the shovel back in the shed. Back inside the garage, I grab the family-sized Igloo cooler off the shelf. The bag of deadweight goes inside, and on top of that, ice from the nearby deep freezer. The whole time, I'm thinking I'll have to scour this thing with bleach later.

As I enter the house, I pause to hear the sound of Jimmy's laughter.

*     *     *

My watch reads 2:32. My new shovel hangs in the shed. The road kill rests in an ice-filled Igloo in the garage. Tooper sleeps on the couch. I stand frozen in the hallway. And Jimmy laughs in his bedroom. At two-thirty.

Jimmy says something and laughs again. My son is talking in his sleep, a regular practice for him. I know that from listening to him during those midnight shots of Jack Daniel's on the couch. But he's speaking in whole sentences. He's talking to *someone*, something he never does at two-thirty.

I stand five steps from Jimmy's closed bedroom door. Glass shards hang from the knees of my sweatpants and who-knows-what germs still cling to my unwashed hands. I should change my clothes and wash my filthy road kill hands, but not yet. I have to hear what he's saying. I have to know if someone's in the house. This can't wait for me to tidy up first.

After a pause, Jimmy talks again, and I inch down the hall, approaching his room with my feet spread from wall to wall. My house is old and full of squeaks. I need to creep up to Jimmy's door and eavesdrop on him without stepping on a noisy floorboard.

Take a step. Okay, good to go. Take another. Good. Now one more. I'm almost there.

Jimmy talks again. "That tickles," he says.

His words send a chill down my back. One more step. My heart threatens to pound through my ribcage.

"You're a good-"

*Squeak.*

I wince at the sound, and Jimmy stops in mid-sentence. I hear him hop off the mattress and pad to the door.

"Dad?"

I peek into his room, but nobody's there. Just his bed, the dresser, dirty clothes, a pile of Legos. "Jimmy, what are you doing?"

"Nothing," he says, and looks at my sweatpants. "Where did you go?"

My mind races. Only insane fathers leave their children at night to scrape road kill off the highway, so I dodge. "Never mind. Who were you talking to?"

They say when people lie, the eyes turn toward the creative part of the brain. Rachel said I always turned my eyes to the right.

Jimmy's eyes circle to his right. "I guess I was talking in my sleep again."

"I know. Who were you *talking* to?"

"Mom."

"You're lying. You weren't talking to her. Now who were you talking to?"

His lower lip quivers and his voice cracks. "I don't know."

"Jimmy-get back in bed. We'll talk in the morning."

"Yes, sir."

I stand by the door and listen for the mattress squeak as he climbs back into bed, then I head to the kitchen.

I'm lying to my son, and my son's lying to me. But I'll sort it out later.

After scrubbing my hands, I reach under the kitchen sink to retrieve the sacred bottle and shot glass. I slump onto the couch, unscrew the cap, and pour a glass, just like every night.

Then she starts in.

*What was our son doing? You know he wasn't talking to me.*

What am I supposed to do, argue about it at two-thirty in the morning? Let me drink in peace, woman.

*But honey, something's wrong. Our son needs you now. He needs you present and sober.*

I've been right here. Where else would I be?

*Have you been here?*

I pause and look at the brown liquid in the shot glass. Point. Jimmy's talking to someone in his sleep and he's lying about it. And I'm scraping road kill off the highway at two in the morning. Maybe something *is* wrong.

*Of course it is. This anniversary was worse than most, for both of you. You don't need this, and neither does he.*

Alright, enough. Look, if I put the booze down, will you get off my back? Will you just shut up and leave me alone?

Silence.

I take one more look at the shot. With a resigned sigh, I rise from the couch and head to the kitchen. I'm about to dump the shot down the drain when I think better of it, down it, and stash the bottle under the sink. Just one shot tonight, to help me sleep. Besides, dumping an entire bottle of Jack Daniel's would be a surer sign of insanity than scraping up road kill at two in the morning.

They say office life is like prison life. Both places lock you into an institutional routine. Both make you cherish privacy above all else. And both make you sit on your rear end for hours, longing for sunlight and fresh air.

It's ironic how a job requiring mental proficiency can include such mind-numbing activity.

I work as a software engineer for a company called Global Industry Cybernet, or GIC for short. Rachel laughed the first time I told her I was a geek for GIK.

The dream sticks to my mind like lint to my chinos. I still see the look on Rachel's face, right after the embolism has taken her life. She asks, *"What about the dog?"*

The dog now sits on ice in the trunk of my rental.

I'm probably insane for bringing it to work in a cooler. Granted, it's in a garbage bag *inside* the cooler, but still...

I use the phone for a personal call. Not too loud, or the warden might hear me. "PetSmart," the perky female voice says.

"Can you guys read RFIDs?"

"RFIDs?"

"Microchips."

"The one in your pet?"

"That's right."

"We don't have a scanner for those. I think the Humane Society has them. You might want to try Hawthorne, too."

The breakfast conversation sticks to my mind as well. I still can't believe what Jimmy said. It has to be a dream. Kids have overactive imaginations, especially him.

Embolisms form because of cholesterol-induced plaque buildups. I have since treated cholesterol as the enemy, staying as far from saturated fats as possible. I enforce bran flakes with soymilk.

At the breakfast table, I pour soymilk into Jimmy's bowl. "I'm going to ask you this one more time. Who were you talking to last night?"

Jimmy's spoon freezes midway to his mouth.

Reply to an email. Sure, I'll attend the analysis meeting. I can think of nowhere else I'd rather be on a Monday at five-thirty.

Jimmy looks at me from under a curtain bang of blonde hair-Rachel's hair. Under his eyes hang bags the size of quarters. He takes a bite and munches in silence for a moment. Finally, he mutters, "Molly."

"What?"

"It's the dog we hit, Dad. Her name's Molly."

A block of ice appears in the pit of my stomach. "What are you talking about?"

Use the mouse and move some binary code to a new file. They want an event-driven application, so hop to it. Get busy. Save the file and don't forget to create a backup. Life is so uncertain.

My spoon drops, splashing soymilk on the table. "What do you mean you *saw* her? Like a ghost?" My own words sound crazy in my ears, and the block of ice gets bigger.

"I don't know. She was *here*, on the bed."

Hearing Jimmy tell an outlandish tale about seeing a dead dog makes me consider the options. There are four explanations: Jimmy's dreaming, he's lying, he's crazy, or...

*Our son is not crazy.*

At work, I get back on the phone. "Hawthorne Animal Hospital," says another female voice, this one scratchy. Dogs bark in the background. Real, live dogs.

"Do you guys have scanners for microchips?"

I stare at my son. "Jimmy, it was a dream. That's it. I don't care what you think you saw. You were dreaming, nothing more, okay?"

"But, Dad-"

"Hey, are you lying to me? Huh?"

"No, sir."

"Are you telling me everything? Are you leaving anything out?"

"No, sir. I really saw Molly-"

"Because if you're not lying, then either you're dreaming or you're crazy. Now which is it?"

"I don't-"

"Huh? Which is it? Are you crazy? Because crazy people see ghosts, Jimmy. Crazy people. Is that what you are?"

"No," he mumbles.

"Then that means you're dreaming, doesn't it?"

"Yes, sir."

I switch to the integrated development environment, my tool of the trade. Sip my coffee and type some more code. If I look busy, the warden might not notice me. At lunchtime, I can leave for my daily hour of exercise and sunlight.

"You want to scan your pet?" asks the Hawthorne employee with the scratchy voice. "Do you have a dog or a cat?"

"It's a dog. I...found her. Can I bring her in?"

At the breakfast table, I give a long sigh and rub my eyes. "Just a dream, Jimmy. Nothing more."

"But she tickled me, Dad."

"What?"

"When she was close, it tickled."

"Jimmy, enough with the ghost story. Finish your breakfast and get to the bus."

While a dead dog rests in a cooler in the car, I sit in front of my computer monitor and question not only my sanity but also that of my son. Is Jimmy crazy?

*Our son is not crazy.*

He believes he saw Molly last night; I hate to admit it but it's true. Is he lying, then? But why would he lie about this?

The clock reads 11:20. Close enough to lunchtime. Get out of here and head to Hawthorne.

*       *       *

I'm talking to the employee at Hawthorne Animal Hospital, and all I can think is, she's cute.

I stand at the front desk of a suburban veterinary clinic. A mélange of pine cleaner disinfectant, animal dander, and urine assaults my nostrils. The air pulses with barking and caterwauling, making conversation difficult. I stand close enough to the front sliding door to breathe an occasional gust of fresh air as new clients enter.

But the malodorous atmosphere doesn't distract me from the good-looking Hawthorne employee behind the counter.

Her nametag reads "Linda." She's fortyish and attractive, and with her eye color, hairstyle, and high cheekbones, she bears a striking resemblance to Michelle Pfeiffer. Tight-jeans. No wedding ring. Maybe she's a divorcee.

*Or maybe she's widow. Maybe her spouse died, too. Did you consider that?*

Linda looks at the closed cooler with genuine sorrow. Her scratchy voice proves she was the one who spoke with me over the phone. "You found the dog on the road?"

"Not exactly. I'm sorry. I know this seems weird."

"No, that's okay."

"I actually *hit* her yesterday."

"Oh, you hit her." She sounds reverent with understanding.

"She came out of nowhere, you know? Jumped right in my path. There was nothing I could do."

"That happens," Linda says, "I grew up on a farm. We ran over squirrels and opossums all the time. Still breaks my heart to hit a dog, though."

Linda stares down at the cooler through curled eyelashes. Carefully applied makeup covers her slight crow's feet around the eyes, while at the same time accentuating her pouting mouth.

*Quit checking out the Hawthorne employee. Remember, you're here to deliver road kill.*

"Sir?"

"Excuse me?"

"You don't know whose dog it is?"

"That's why I want to scan her. Maybe we can find out who the owner is."

"So you can take her back?" Linda's eyes crinkle with heartfelt admiration. "That's sweet."

I nod while assuming my humblest smile. What else can I do, admit I'm doing this because my dead wife told me to?

"What about the collar?" Linda says. "Doesn't she have a dog tag?"

"She does, but it's scratched up beyond recognition."

"We can take her and scan her, if you like."

Linda's eyes meet mine, but I look back down at the cooler.

Other terms for the phrase *moving on* are to *advance*, to *progress*, or to *evolve*. Rachel won't let me do any of those.

Still gazing at the cooler, I say, "That would be great. Thank you."

"No problem. It'll be a day or two. We'll call you and let you know."

I beat a hasty retreat, hoping deep down that Linda's the one who calls me back.

This evening, while Jimmy plays video games on the living room floor, I sit on the couch sipping coffee and reading Popular Mechanics. Amidst flashes of gunfire on the television screen and sounds of alien death from the speakers, I immerse myself in an article on six-engine icebreaker ships in Antarctica. They actually coat the hulls with slippery paint to slide through glaciers. Interesting.

A subwoofer explosion breaks my reverie. "Boy, turn that down, *now*."

"Yes, sir," he mumbles, and grabs for the remote.

Try as I may, I can't get back into the article. My mind wanders, considering the options: Jimmy's dreaming, he's lying, he's crazy, or he's experiencing the paranormal truth. I'm almost convinced he's not dreaming. I don't want to think he's crazy. He has nothing to gain from lying about this. And I can't possibly accept option four.

*You might have to accept it, honey. What other choices are there?*

Weariness covers me like an iceberg. Last night's road kill rescue, along with today's lunch errand to the vet, has sapped my remaining energy. Plus, there's the dream that haunts me, and the ghost that haunts Jimmy.

What am I saying? It could be anything: a bad dream, something he ate, an overactive imagination, anything.

I keep telling myself that. But I know he's not dreaming. And I don't know why he'd lie to me. And he doesn't show any symptoms of madness.

*Our son is not crazy. You hear my voice, don't you? Is it that much of a stretch for our son to see Molly?*

Are there more than just those four options? No. What else could it be? Jimmy believes he played with Molly last night, and she was here with him. He *wasn't* dreaming; he was awake when I came in. That leaves his insanity or an insane truth, both undesirable outcomes.

*Our son is not crazy. Crazy people exhibit other signs: paranoia, convulsions, eating disorders, nervous ticks. You've seen it in movies and on television talk shows. He shows none of that.*

Yeah, but crazy people see ghosts, don't they?

*Do crazy people hear them, honey?*

Tooper hops onto the couch and hobbles to my lap. I lift the magazine above her to keep the appearance of reading, and her purring vibrates my legs.

*Our son hears things at night. He sees and plays with a dead dog. Why don't you discuss it with him?*

No way. I'm not encouraging this fantasy. He has to learn to grow up and face reality.

*What he sees and feels is as real as I am to you right now.*

I ponder this as I sip my coffee. Suddenly, Tooper's purring stops. She goes rigid in my lap, digging her claws through my jeans and making me spill my coffee.

"What in the world?" Coffee seeps into the magazine, my jeans, and the carpet.

"What is it?" Jimmy pauses the game to look.

Tooper jumps off my lap, arches her back, and hisses at something near the door to the garage. The block of ice forms in my stomach again. What is going on? The cat's gaze turns toward Jimmy, and she crouches and growls in his direction.

I gawk at her, but Jimmy smiles. "Oh, she's here."

The block of ice grows and deepens, sliding into my bowels. My heart gives one, solid thump before sticking in my throat. "What?"

"She's here."

"Who's here?"

"Molly. She's right here."

*Surreal* is the closest word that comes to mind. Whatever it is, I can't see it, but Jimmy and Tooper sure can. Their gazes follow it to a spot next to me on the couch.

"She's right next to you," Jimmy says, pointing.

I feel nothing except a flash of heat in my neck. I see nothing except my arm hairs rising.

Out of instinct, I leap off my seat, sending the magazine and coffee cup to the floor. Immediately embarrassed, I lash out. "Jimmy, *enough* with the ghost thing. No more ghosts. Look, nothing's there." I bat my hand above the couch cushions.

"But, Dad-"

"No. This is ridiculous."

With one final growl, Tooper lunges at the couch, and I flinch. She hits the cushion, rebounds off it, and retreats down the hall to the master bedroom.

"What the-"

"She bit Tooper, Dad."

"What do you mean she bit Tooper?"

"Tooper was right there and-"

"She did *not*..." I stop and silently count to five. This is getting nowhere.

I want to accuse him of lying, of dreaming, of making this whole thing up in his little overactive head, but I can't ignore the situation. Something inexplicable happened.

*Maybe it's time to tell our son about the road kill rescue.*

"Do you still see her?"

"Yes, sir."

"Describe her."

"She's skinny, like a greyhound or something, but tan."

"It was a whippet. We hit a whippet."

"What's a whippet, Dad?"

"Never mind. Forget about it. This is insane."

"There she goes," Jimmy says, following invisible motion with his eyes.

"What?"

"She's heading to the garage."

"Alright, Jimmy, enough with the ghost thing." I take a deep breath. "Turn the game off and go to bed."

"Yes, sir."

*And maybe it's time to talk to our son about why he and Tooper can see, but you can't.*

I'm still coming to grips with *what* he's seeing. If he's seeing *anything*.

\*        \*        \*

Let me make this perfectly clear: I don't believe in ghosts. By the way, Rachel's not a ghost, not in the strictest sense. It's different when it's your wife. That's another thing altogether.

When you grow up in a Baptist family, you don't believe in ghosts, goblins, vampires, or anything else supernatural, except for what's in the Bible, of course. All those whackos who claim to see dead people roaming their houses or to hear chains rattling in their basements just make me laugh.

Well, they *used* to make me laugh.

The Bible never mentions ghosts, except for the Holy Ghost, but that's different. Then there's that one time the Israelite king summoned the spirit of an old prophet, but that's it, that's the only reference. Seeing ghosts was the exception, not the rule.

I decide to shoot straight with Jimmy, to tell him the truth about the road kill rescue. Maybe it'll help him understand what he's seeing, so he'll know it's *not* a ghost. And maybe if I do, Rachel will get off my back about it.

At the dinner table, I pass the macaroni and cheese. "I'm not saying I believe in ghosts or anything," I start saying, "But, you know the other night, when you talked in your sleep?"

Jimmy globs a mountain of macaroni onto his plate and nods.

My throat feels dry, so I take a drink of soymilk. "There was a reason I was fully dressed at two in the morning."

"There was?" he says past a bite of food.

"Yes. I got Molly. I took her off the road and put her in the cooler."

Jimmy's mouth hangs open and exposes a half-chewed nibble of dinner.

"It's what your mother would have wanted."

"Yeah."

To this day, I have never told Jimmy about Rachel's presence after death, but I think he suspects. "Yesterday, I took her to the vet to see if they could scan her microchip, so maybe we can find out who the owner is."

"Why?"

"I want to take her back."

Jimmy's eyes grow as big as half-dollars. "You do?"

"Yeah," I say nonchalantly. "Like I said, it's what your mother would have wanted. So, the vet called me back today." I didn't add that it wasn't Linda. "And-"

"Did they find Molly's home?"

"Will you let me finish?"

Jimmy buttoned his lip.

"Anyway, the owner's Jane Robinson, but the address is an old house on Keebler. Nobody's been there for years." I pause. I don't really want to reveal the next part, but it's the honest-to-God truth, no way around it. "And the dog's name is Molly."

Jimmy beams. "It is? Wow."

A silence falls between us, and I welcome it. Something strange is transpiring in this family, and my mind still hasn't absorbed it all.

I take a deep breath and put both hands on the table. "Jimmy, I don't know what's happening here. We don't believe in ghosts. Period. Something else is going on, something bad. Tell me exactly what you saw last night."

"In the living room?"

"Yes. What did you see?"

Jimmy screws his little face in concentration. "She was just there, all of a sudden."

"There?" I point at the door to the garage.

"Yeah, and she looked wet."

"Wet? What do you mean?"

"Shiny, like with water."

What does that mean? I'm no psychologist, but that doesn't sound like any delusional vision I've ever heard of. "Okay, then what happened?"

"She walked over there," he says, pointing to the living room, "and jumped on the couch."

"Did you hear her? Smell her?" I shake my head in disbelief. "Jimmy, I didn't feel anything on the couch next to me. Got it? I'm not believing any of this."

Jimmy's lower lip quivers. "I saw her," he mumbles.

"I know you think you saw her, but you didn't, okay? There are no ghosts, Jimmy. None. I don't know what you saw, or what happened last night, but it wasn't a ghost. Got it?"

Jimmy's eyes glisten, and I get up from the table and storm off to my workshop in the garage.

This is nuts. There are no ghosts. We live in reality, not fantasy.

*But what happens when reality collides with your preconceptions, honey?*

Don't you start in on me. You're already dead. This is not your concern.

*Oh, yes it is. He's my son, too.*

The door creaks open, and Jimmy shuffles out. "Dad, did you bring Molly back?"

"Get back inside, Jimmy."

"But Dad, is she here?"

"Yeah, why?"

"Can-can I see her?"

"No."

"Please, Dad?"

"I *said...*" I take a deep breath. I suppose there's no harm in showing him the road kill. He's already seen it. "Alright, get over here."

The frosty air pours out of the deep freezer as I hold it open. Jimmy peers inside at a piece of plastic-wrapped road kill as if it's buried treasure.

"That's her," Jimmy whispers.

"I wrapped her up. She should last a while, a week, maybe two. Long enough for us to find her home."

"She's real."

"This is real, Jimmy. The road kill. Not what you're seeing."

*Face it, honey. This might just be another exception to the rule.*

I stand in the garage with my son and ponder my moral dilemma. Jimmy claims to see things I've always believed weren't possible. I've never believed in ghosts, never believed in anything supernatural except for what's in the Bible. Except for God.

*But the proof's right here. You saw what Tooper did last night. And Jimmy knew the name Molly before the vet called.*

So maybe he's psychic or something. Did you think of that?

*And honey, how do you know this isn't God's way of breaking through to you?*

That settles it. I make up my mind to call Hank Larson, the church counselor. He'll help me sort out this mess.

"Alright, we're letting out the cold air." I shut the lid. "Back inside."

"Yes, sir."

*     *     *

The night of Tooper's couch-attack is only one of many bizarre episodes. Now Jimmy claims to see Molly all the time, and it drives me nuts.

I call Hank Larson at the First Baptist Church to make an appointment to see him. He's booked for the next couple of days, but how does seven o'clock Friday evening sound?

On the night after I tell Jimmy about the road kill rescue, I'm having the Rachel dream again when I wake up to hear my son giggling in his bedroom. The next morning, he tells me Molly tickled him. He claims she visits him every night now and tickles him when she's close.

On Friday, I tell Jimmy I have a date and hire a babysitter to watch him. I don't want him knowing about my visit to the church counselor.

I park the Ford rental in the church parking lot and get out. There's an icy November wind tonight, and it bites to the bone. I race inside from the cold to the relative warmth of the church foyer, shake off my leather coat, and head to Hank's office, just to the right down the hall.

Hank sits patiently at his desk. He greets me, invites me to sit down, and closes the door. "How's it going?"

"Pretty good," I say, and then shake my head in disbelief at my own lie. "Not really."

I'm sure it's not coincidental that Jimmy tends to see Molly right after we talk about her. One morning as Jimmy heads to the school bus, I tell him, "Hey, enough with the Molly stories at night. There are no such things as ghosts, understand?"

"Yes, sir," he says, and then looks near the garage door. "Whoa. I don't think she liked it when you said that, Dad."

Sitting in Hank's office, I remember he's no stranger to suffering. He's a counselor who's been there and has the scars to show for it. He's a widower, like me, whose wife died in a commuter accident a decade earlier. On his desk is a picture of his rebellious son I know hasn't spoken to him in at least four years. Speaking of scars, a tumor scar stretches down the left side of his neck, looking like someone carved a section of his jaw line away.

Suffering chases this man like nightmares chase me, so when he sits in that chair and gives counsel, I'm confident he knows what he's talking about. Besides, if anyone can help me get my dead wife out of my head, he can.

Hank's disfigured jaw line stretches in a smile. "It's been a while since we had a session. How's that lizard treating you?"

He always refers to my bouts of depression as a lizard creeping up on me. All I have to do is flick it off. "That's not why I'm here tonight. I need to talk about something else."

"What's going on?"

Sometimes Jimmy says Molly plays with him while we're outside. On one Saturday afternoon, Jimmy and I rake the oak leaves in the front yard.

"Dad, shouldn't we chop this tree down?" Jimmy points to the fifty-year-old oak tree by the bedroom window, split down the middle like a peeled banana. "It's ugly."

"Someday."

Jimmy drops his rake. "Whoa."

"What?"

"Molly's here. She's chasing the leaves."

The wind catches some oak leaves, and I look at Jimmy and wonder why he's doing this to me.

I give Hank Larson a hard look. "You're going to think I'm crazy."

"No I won't. You might have unresolved-grief-induced melancholy, but you're not crazy."

"Thanks. That makes me feel loads better."

Another twisted jaw line smile. "What's up?"

"It's about Jimmy."

"Oh?"

"Wait. Let me back up. You know we were in an accident last Sunday?"

"No. Is everyone okay?"

"Everyone's fine, thank goodness, but we hit a dog. She ran out in front of us, and then we got rear ended."

"Ouch."

"Yeah, and you know what day that was."

Hank pauses. "That was the anniversary of Rachel's death. Oh, man, I'm sorry."

"It's alright, but you know, that just made things worse. The Honda's totaled, by the way."

"I did notice you were driving a different car. Didn't think you liked Fords."

"True. It's a rental. Anyway, since then, Jimmy's been seeing things."

"Like what?"

I pause and take a deep breath. How's Hank going to take this? "He says he's been seeing a ghost."

I place an ad in the local paper. It reads, "FOUND @ S.159 (11/5), Molly, female tan whippet, medium sz, black collar, microchip." After that, I leave my phone number. I don't have the guts to mention I ran her over then scraped her off the highway and stored her in my deep freezer. These are facts I think should be delivered in person.

At ten cents per character, the ad costs me $9.75. The vet charges me $35.66 for scanning the microchip and for storing Molly overnight. The totaling of my new Honda represents a loss of $22,753.38. And Hank charges me $46.50 for the counseling visit. So far, the road kill I want to return to its owner costs me $22,845.29.

And of course, not a soul responds to my ad. Go figure.

"Has he told you he's been seeing a ghost?" Hank asks.

"Yes, but there's more. Weird things have been happening."

"What kind of things?"

Then I relate the entire story to Hank. I tell him about the accident and about the road kill rescue, saying it's what Rachel would have wanted. I tell him about Jimmy claiming to see Molly at night and about our recent conversations. I tell him about Tooper's couch-attack and the vet's findings. I leave out the dream of my deceased wife; I want Hank to think I'm making *some* progress.

"Have you ever thought Jimmy might be making this up? He might be lying."

"Of course I have. From the beginning, I've thought there were four options. He's dreaming, he's lying, he's crazy, or he's telling the truth."

*Our son is not crazy, remember? And he wouldn't lie about this.*

After a thoughtful silence, Hank says, "I'm not a psychologist. I'm not the person to look into your son's head and tell you what's wrong."

"I don't think he's crazy, Hank. He doesn't show any other signs of that."

"There's crazy, and then there's crazy. With his mom dead and his dad suffering from depression, then this accident, it all adds up. And again, how do you know he isn't just making this up?"

"I think he's doing just that, but the question is why?"

"I don't know. To get your attention, maybe? Regardless, so far all you've mentioned are things that could be happening in his head alone. They might not be real."

That gives me pause. I reflect on the events of the past week. Jimmy talking in his sleep, seeing Molly in the house, playing with Molly outside, feeling tickled when Molly's near. It's entirely my son's imagination.

"True," I say. "How can I explain the cat's reaction the other night?"

"Could be anything. Maybe she smelled the dog on you. You'd been handling it recently."

I did sit on that couch after the road kill rescue, debating whether to drink or not, talking to Rachel. Maybe Tooper just smelled Molly on the upholstery. I nod my head.

"Think about it," Hank says. "Combine a child's imagination with the stress of recent events, and you have yourself a ghost."

"Yeah, that's what I thought, too." His words carry the confident ring of truth and confirm my suspicions. Still, something in the back of my mind still bugs me. "One more thing. Jimmy knew Molly's name before the vet told me. Do you think he's, I don't know, psychic or something?"

He pauses a moment. "Maybe that's the point where God's stepping in here. You can't discount that."

"Maybe."

"You have to ask yourself, what does God want to teach me in this situation?"

I nod. Has Rachel been talking to him, too?

Hank stands and slaps my shoulder. "You head back home with your son, and I'll pray for you, okay?"

"Alright, thanks."

*       *       *

I watch the days pass by, waiting for someone to respond to my newspaper ad. I even look in the white pages under Robinson, hoping for a different address besides the house on Keebler. Unfortunately, Robinsons fill three quarters of a page, and none of them is Jane.

I also explain to Rachel how I'm trying to find Molly's owner, really trying, and will this make her happy? Will she just get out of my head once I return the road kill? It's been a week since I took a drink. Doesn't that count for something?

Finally fed up with waiting for responses to my ad, I decide to visit the address from Molly's microchip.

On a gray Wednesday evening, right after dinner, I take Jimmy with me on a drive to Keebler. Maybe I'll learn something about Molly's owner. Then again, maybe I won't even be able to get in.

I drive the Ford rental through residential suburbia. People rake leaves in their front yards, making little piles close to the road. It's a quiet drive.

*Talk to our son, honey.*

"How was school today?"

"Okay. Molly came with me."

I sigh. "Jimmy, what have I told you about that?"

"But she sits on the floor next to my desk."

"No, she *doesn't*. Molly's road kill. Road kill doesn't sit next to you in class."

"But, Dad-"

"Enough. If you have anything to say besides 'I saw a ghost in school today,' I'll hear it. Otherwise, just keep quiet."

More silence. Are you happy? This is why I don't talk to Jimmy these days.

I turn onto Keebler and slow down to find the house. There it is, Number 11, tucked away on the left. I pull into the gravel driveway and park.

At first, I just sit and gaze at the disarray before me. The house itself is quaint, a half-brick ranch-style in decent condition. The yard looks quite the opposite. It looks like a prairie restoration project: two-foot-high wheat grass sways in the autumn breeze, and lilac bushes gone to seed clog the front picture window. Weed colonies poke through the gravel driveway, some reaching above the hood of the car. A RE/MAX sign stands half-hidden in the grass next to the rusty mailbox.

"Wow," Jimmy says. "It's like a haunted house."

"Yeah, whatever. Come on."

I get out and walk around the weeds up the driveway. Jimmy opens his door and follows. A woman rakes leaves next door with her kids, and she waves at us. I return the wave, self-conscious and trying not to attract too much attention.

Jimmy gasps. "Oh, she came with us!" He laughs and races through the waving grass. The woman next door notices my son and studies him. I grin and laugh it off. She probably thinks I'm the parent of a special-needs kid.

I approach the house on a cobblestone walkway that cuts a swath through the prairie grass. Weeds creep between the stones. A gray key box hangs from the front door handle. What do I plan to do, barge on in? I lean over some lilac branches as much as possible to peer into the picture window. Darkness inside, nothing else.

What was I thinking, coming here? There's nothing to see, no clues leading me to Molly's owner.

"It's over by the mailbox," someone says.

"Excuse me?"

It's the woman next-door, standing on her side of the chain link fence. She's a good-looking, middle-aged redhead, with faded jeans and a sweatshirt. "The real estate agent's contact sheets. They're over there." She points to the RE/MAX sign.

"Oh, right. Thanks."

"She was a sweet lady, Mrs. Robinson."

"You knew her?"

"Sure did." She brushes leaves off her jeans with her raking gloves. "Her and her husband built that house in 1956. It was the first one in the neighborhood. It's just sad to see it go like this."

Her kids run through the yard behind her, filling the air with squeals. Her son, who looks about four, chases his little sister around the yard with a twig in his hand, grunting like a gorilla.

"Just like mine," I say, and upon seeing her puzzled look, I add, "I have an older home as well. You know, I think it was the first house, too."

"That's something."

"Yeah. So, I guess she passed on?"

The mom nods. "Five years ago. She left the house to her daughter. Kate lived her for a while, but then she moved last spring."

"Kate?"

"Her daughter. I think she got a job in St. Louis."

"Okay." I try not to sound too interested, try not to betray the pounding of my heart. I want to ask urgent questions. Did Jane have a tan-colored whippet named Molly? Where does Kate live? Has she been looking for her mom's dog? But I can't just ask a stranger these things. My being here already feels too awkward.

Jimmy's still running through the overgrown weeds, chasing who-knows-what. The neighbor's kids frolic through the leaves in their yard.

"They love yard work," the mom says with a grin.

"I can tell," I say with a chuckle. This woman isn't half-bad looking. With her raking gloves, I can't see if there's a ring or not.

*What did you come here to do, track down Molly's home or check out the neighbor?*

"What's your boy doing?" she asks.

"Oh, Jimmy? He, uh, he loves tall grass. We have an apartment, and the landlord must mow that lawn twice a week."

"Oh." She nods, and then looks puzzled. "I thought you had the first home in your neighborhood?"

Crap. "Uh, yeah, the complex *was* the first building, actually. So how much is she asking for it?"

"I don't know. It's all right there on the sheet." She points again to the RE/MAX sign. "Are you thinking of buying?"

"Yeah, I'm looking. Well, thanks a lot for your time."

"No problem." She smiles and returns to her yard work.

I step through the weeds to pluck a realtor sheet from the stack below the RE/MAX sign. "Jimmy, we're going."

"Yes, sir," he says as we hop back into the Ford rental.

I glance over the sheet as we drive through the neighborhood. The list price for the house shows in bold at the top. Below that is the name and number of the agent, Susan Banks, RE/MAX Real Estate Consultant. And below that, under "Seller," appears the name Kate Robinson. That's it. No address or phone number. They clearly want prospective buyers to go through the real estate agent.

Jimmy looks at the sheet. "What's that, Dad?"

"Another dead end."

At least I have a name, though: Kate Robinson.

*     *     *

More days pass. Rachel's still in my head, gnawing away at my conscience, though I've been sober for two weeks and I've been busting my tail trying to return the road kill to its owner. Still nobody responds to my newspaper ad, and the lack of responses only hardens my resolve to find the owner. I want to get rid of this dog, to rid myself of the road kill in the deep freezer, but I can't get myself to bury it or pitch it in a dumpster. Such a dismissal would never satisfy my conscience (a.k.a. Rachel).

So, I obtain a St. Louis phone book and look for Kate Robinson, but she's not there. I find only Karen and Kevin, not even a K. Robinson. They haven't updated the white pages since Jane's daughter moved to the city, I suppose.

I call Susan Banks, the RE/MAX real estate agent, and the conversation is predictable:

"RE/MAX. Susan Banks."

"Good afternoon. I'm calling about the house for sale on Keebler, Number 11?"

"Number 11 Keebler." Papers rustle. "Here it is. How can I help you?"

"Actually, I was wondering if I could contact the seller directly. I believe it's Kate Robinson?"

A brief pause. "Sir, unfortunately, we're not allowed to give out personal information without the seller's approval."

"I understand. Thanks anyway."

And that's that. I can think of nothing else to do at this point. I even try searching for Kate Robinson on the internet, but come up with a multitude of irrelevant results. All this searching only makes me feel like a stalker, and I can't even find anything.

Jimmy's not sleeping much at night, looking haggard as we eat breakfast each morning. He says he plays with Molly, that she wakes him up and tickles him. Hearing these things and seeing him like this simultaneously makes me want to smack him and hug him. My son's obsessed with a lie, with something he believes is true but can't be true, and it's taking its toll on him. And his lying is taking its toll on me.

And Rachel keeps telling me to say something to him, to *do* something.

But what can I do? I'm not a shrink; I'm a software engineer. All I have to go on is instinct and logic, and my instinct tells me if I return the road kill, this will all go away. And logic tells me finding Molly's owner is the key. Everything will work out when I return her to Kate Robinson.

The following Saturday morning, while Jimmy watches cartoons, I sip coffee at the dining room table and catch up on my Popular Mechanics. Molly's the last thing on my mind as I return to the article on icebreaker ships in

Antarctica. Sometimes the vessels encounter century-old icebergs, and it takes weeks for the bows to pierce through-

Jimmy leaps to his feet. "Whoa!"

"What now?"

On the television is a commercial for the St. Louis Zoo. Raja the elephant lumbers across a pseudo-Serengeti landscape.

"Okay, okay." Jimmy kneels and pets empty air in front of him.

"Jimmy, what are you doing?"

"It's Molly, Dad. She wants to go to the zoo."

"Hey, what did I say? There is no Molly."

"The commercial came on, and she jumped around."

"Jimmy, Molly is road kill in the freezer."

"She really wants to go." Jimmy looks at me with pleading eyes. "Can we go, Dad?"

"First, no, we're not going anywhere you want to go because of a ghost. There are no ghosts and there is no Molly, understand?" I glance out the window at the November grayness. "And second, it's forty degrees outside and looks like rain. No way. Now shut up about Molly, alright?"

"We can wear our coats."

"What did I say? There are no ghosts, and we're not going to the zoo. End of story."

"But Dad-"

"That's it." Smack goes the magazine onto the coffee table, and I'm on my feet. "Jimmy, I've had it up to my eyeballs with all this Molly talk. Enough. Not another word."

"Dad, you're not listening. Molly-"

My footsteps thunder across the living room floor. "You better shut your mouth, boy, or I'll shut it for you."

"But what if Molly's the only-"

"*Shut up!*" The hand comes down before I know it, and I cuff Jimmy across the cheek. The blow sends him crashing across the coffee table and onto the floor. "Just like your mother. You don't know when to *shut up!*"

Jimmy lays there in a heap, between the couch and the coffee table.

"This is over, *now*, do you hear?"

His head creeps up, and his mouth hangs open, letting blood seep onto the tabletop. With a soft clink, a tooth falls. His eyes gape at it.

I grab my hair with both hands. "*Why* did you make me do that? Why didn't-"

With that, Jimmy bolts up and races to his room. The door slams.

*What have you done?*

Not now, woman. Not now.

I stand there in the living room, still feeling the sting of my son's cheek on the back of my hand. Jimmy's sobs erupt from his bedroom.

Why did he make me do that? Why didn't he just shut up about the dog, that stupid dog?

Despite my anger over the dog obsession, my veins fill with ice at the sight of Jimmy's bloody tooth on the coffee table. What have I done? What have I been doing?

*       *       *

I spend practically the rest of the day in the garage workshop. The first half of the Jack Daniel's is gone before noon, and the whole bottle's almost finished before I lose track of time.

The image keeps playing in my mind. The smack. The fall. The bloody tooth. And all over a stupid dog.

And Rachel won't let up on me.

*Do you realize what you've done?*

What do you think, woman? I did it, didn't I?

*And you call yourself a father.*

Get off my back, will you?

*No! You get back in there and love him as a real father would.*

Nothing you say could send me back in there, so just get off my back.

But I'm doing more than drinking myself stupid and arguing with my dead wife; I keep myself busy. I retrieve the frozen road kill from the deep freezer, place it in a cardboard box, and reinforce the seals with layers of duct tape. After that, I store the box in the trunk of the Ford rental. Molly's been here long enough; it's time for her to go. I don't care if it's a ditch or a dumpster. She's not staying here another night.

One thing stops me from starting the car, though. Since I won't be returning the road kill to its owner, maybe this won't all go away. What if Jimmy still claims to see Molly? That won't do. I want this to end now, and that means he needs to know it's over, and that means he needs to do this with me.

The house is a jerky blur, but somehow I end up in front of Jimmy's bedroom door.

"Jimmy, get out here. Time to go."

No answer.

"I said, get out here. We're leaving."

Still no answer, so I open the door. The room's empty. Just the bed, his dresser, some dirty clothes, that same pile of Legos. "Jimmy?"

The curtains flutter, and I feel the cool breeze through the window. He's gone.

*Great. Look at what you've done. You've chased our son away.*

Shut up. Not now.

My mind's cloudy enough with the booze, too cloudy to think. A burning anger rises like boiling blood up my torso and neck. Jimmy left. He just stepped right out the window and left. What the heck does he think he's going to do? Where's he going to go?

*Where would he go? Where did he say he would go? Think.*

I race through the house, search my bedroom, the bathroom, the kitchen. "*Jimmy?*"

I stumble through the front door, hitting a wall of frosty November air, and trip over the threshold onto the porch. It's freezing, and all I have on is my jeans and t-shirt from this morning. "*Jimmy?*" He's not in the front yard. I'm up, I'm going around the side of the house. "Jimmy? Where are you?" By this time, a next-door neighbor raking his leaves glares at me, but I don't care. I make a full circuit of the house, but Jimmy's nowhere in sight.

Where did he go? School? A friend's house? Shouldn't I call the police? The image of Jimmy's bloody tooth makes me cringe. No, the police are out.

*Don't you remember? Where did he want you to take him?*

Through the murky waves of inebriation, one word rises to the surface: zoo.

I trip three times in my dash across the yard and into the garage to reach the car.

*     *     *

I'm driving to the St. Louis Zoo in the Ford, and I'm thinking, am I going to die?

The trip is a blur. I've driven drunk before, but not this drunk. A few beers during happy hour might slow your response time a tad, but your decision-making still works.

Not today. Everything's in slow motion: my driving, the passing landscape, my words, my thoughts. I drive with obsessive caution, only aware of the immediate surroundings. Steering wheel, dashboard, bumper of the car in front of me.

My mind wanders to Jimmy. When did he leave? This morning? An hour ago? And how did he get anywhere? What did he do, hitch a ride? There's public transportation, but how much money does he have? And did he even go to the zoo?

Somewhere a car horn blares at me, and I return my focus to the immediate. Just drive. Just get there.

I arrive at the zoo and somehow make it to a parking spot right across from the south entrance. I'm out, and it's still freezing. Never mind that now. Start running. Cross the road. Pass the two-story concrete blocks that spell Z-O-O. Through the turnstiles. My feet pound the blacktop path.

The place is slow for a Saturday afternoon. In fact, it's empty. It's forty degrees, and the wind knifes me in the face and neck and carries a crisp odor of elephant. What am I doing? I don't know where Jimmy is, if he's even *here*. Wait. He has a maroon coat. I'll keep looking for a maroon coat.

Having something of a plan, I sprint for the middle of the park, toward the sea lions. I'll start there and work my way outward. Just keep going. Keep looking. Look left. There are the bear caves. Look right. Here's a deserted lemonade vendor. Go under an arching sign for a new penguin exhibit. Pass the Children's Zoo. Cross some train tracks. Interrupt a group of autumn walkers, the only souls in the park. "Excuse," I slur. They dodge me, offering offended looks as I pass.

Keep going. See a maroon coat? No. How about over there? No. Keep moving. Head to the middle of the park. And that's when I hear baying and barking ahead. It's feeding time for the sea lions. Turn a corner past an empty information booth, and there it is: a vast open area with a fenced-in pool in the center. Strewn through the pool are rocks on which sit slippery, hungry sea lions.

There are only two people in sight: a woman in a zoo uniform standing by the fence, and next to her, a small figure in a maroon coat.

"*Jimmy!*" I stumble over something, get back up, and head toward them. Both heads turn to me.

The woman's a blonde and the uniform's forest green with ball cap, rubber gloves, and high-water boots. Her blonde ponytail sticks out the back of the ball cap. As I approach, Jimmy calls out to me, but the woman takes a step toward him and slightly in front. A hand goes to his shoulder. Who is this lady?

"Jimmy, what are you doing?" I'm standing in front of them, and that's when I notice his face. His nostrils have little brown plugs of dried blood, and his right cheek is swollen with a stormy bruise.

"Dad?"

The woman just glares at me, and suddenly words are difficult. "Jimmy, where...how did you...?"

"I took the bus, Dad. It's alright." He hooks a little thumb at the woman. "Guess who she is?"

I look her up and down. Other than some hot blonde, I have no clue. I shake my head. "I don't know. Who are you?"

"Kate Robinson." Her words are glacial.

"What? You're..." My mind reels, and I face Jimmy. "How did you know?"

"*She* took me here, Dad. She's her owner." Again, pointing to Kate Robinson.

"Jimmy," I start saying, but that's all that comes out. Wait a second. The thoughts are slow in coming, but when they arrive, they're a thunderclap in my head. Molly led him here. Molly led him to her owner. Either Jimmy has a gift, or...

...and the realization does more to sober me than a gallon of espresso.

"It's true, Dad," Jimmy continues. "She took me here, and then she disappeared. She's gone."

Suddenly, I'm on my knees in front of Jimmy. "Come here." Kate Robinson moves a protective hand to block Jimmy, but he maneuvers around her. I grip his little head, study his cheek, his nose, the damage I did. My vision blurs again, but not from alcohol. I feel a tear come down.

That's all the invitation Jimmy needs. His head is on my chest, and his tiny arms wrap around my neck. This is heaven, right here, right now, and nothing else exists, not Molly, not the cool looks from Kate, not Rachel's voice, nothing.

# Backstage

By Jennifer Shew

*1927*

Lily lifted the delicate necklace from its nest of tissue paper and draped it around her throat, remembering the words of caution against it. She stared into the mirror and sighed, then clasped the necklace and stood up from the vanity, avoiding the reflection of her reflection in the three-way mirror.

A knock on the door startled her from her reverie. "Five minutes, Lily," said the stage manager, his brogue muffled through the clapboard door. The whooshing noise of the restless audience was audible too, mixed with the chirping of cicadas from the nearby park.

"Thanks, Mr. Raeon," she said, belatedly, hearing the stage manager's footsteps fade as he walked away. Doubts assailed her, but in the end she kept the jewelry around her neck. "Opening night," she said softly to herself, patting the necklace. "Don't let history repeat itself."

*Present*

"Quit thinking and start doing," Isabella Carter had muttered to herself before auditioning for the Muny's summer season. And so she had done. She remembered staring a little goggle-eyed at the bulletin board, wondering if she was really seeing her name next to the words "lead actress." She blinked and shook her head, stepping backwards. She touched a finger to the piece of paper, then whirled and ran out of the building.

"I got it!" she had yelled, then covered her mouth with her hands, embarrassed to have shouted her joy to the parking lot. She had brushed past a man standing on the steps on the way to her car, gathering an impression of youth, of dark hair and shining eyes. She stopped just before reaching her battered Saturn, a waft of spices turning her head back toward the steps. The man was staring at her, she thought, and she dropped her gaze briefly. When she looked up, he was gone, but the scent remained. Bella had shaken her head, wondering if her euphoria was giving her delusions.

*     *     *

Right now, Bella wished she was simply imagining things. Rehearsals were twice a week, and every other Saturday. It was a demanding schedule for someone working full-time as Bella did, and she knew it was affecting her performance. She had thought she was handling it rather well, until tonight's endless rehearsal. The director was currently in the midst of a rather colorful tirade at her ineptitude, even going so far as to throw down his clipboard in frustration, shocking the entire cast with his vehemence.

"I picked you for the lead, Isabella, because I thought you had potential. You fit the idea of the playwright's heroine perfectly, so I said, 'What the hell, give her a chance.' But you are not giving me anything, Miss Carter. You are so distracted I wonder that you can learn your lines at all. Your inattention to the blocking is messing up the other actors. Where is the emotion you showed at the audition?" the director asked, scrubbing his hands through his thinning hair. He glanced at the clock and sighed, and Bella blinked away tears.

"You look extremely tired, Isabella. I want you to go home tonight and get some rest. And I want you to think about what's important to you right now. Because this obviously isn't it," he continued, his voice low, disappointed.

He looked up from Isabella and directed his next words to the cast in general. "It's late. We're not getting anywhere with this scene. Everyone go home, sleep, and come back next time ready to work." He squatted down to pick up his clipboard as people shuffled off the hardwood stage. He straightened, only to see Bella still rooted to the spot where she had been standing earlier, her mouth open in a moue of disbelief and pain. She met the director's eyes for a moment, then ran backstage with a sob.

"You need to find a new costume, too," he yelled after her. "You don't look ethereal enough..."

*    *    *

"What was I thinking, trying this..." she said to herself, staring at her reflection in the mirror. The only person she noticed during her headlong run was Harry Raeon, the stage manager, who stared after her with an unfathomable expression, his hands full of microphones. At the beginning of rehearsals, Bella had been surprised to see he was the same man she encountered after her audition, and pleased that he hadn't been a delusion after all. He was nice, handsome in a old-fashioned manner, perhaps just a few years older than herself, but he was crew, and cast and crew didn't mix. Now Bella ignored him, unwilling to let herself see the sympathy in his eyes. She had climbed the circuitous stairs to the green room, heedless of the makeup and costume folks bustling around her. Once upstairs, she took a seat in front of one of the makeup stations, denying the tears burning her eyes and instead looking dazedly at the activity behind her.

Eventually the room cleared, with one bare bulb over the door competing with the vanity lights. A rustle from the racks of costumes drew Bella's attention, and she saw the costume master emerging from the tightly packed outfits, her neon leggings glowing under the fluorescent bulbs.

"Oh, hi, Bella," Anastasia said, smiling. "I didn't know anyone was still here."

"Hmm. Yeah, Stasi, still here. Just been wondering what I've gotten myself into and most likely what I'm about to get out of," Bella said, only a little bitter.

Anastasia dumped her armful of costumes on the table next to Isabella and pulled up a chair, sitting backwards. She reached a hand out to Bella and patted her shoulder. "Look," she said, "I know that this director can be a pain. I've worked with him before. But he knows what he's doing, and he saw something he liked in you when you tried out. I know you've been doing a lot in addition to this, and most people here wouldn't dream of that.

"Just...take his advice, get some more sleep, and take a look at some of these. We could hear him up here, you know. I don't think he realizes how loud he is. I found some things that might be more what he's looking for," she said, gesturing at the pile of fabric beside her. Bella couldn't even begin to figure out what sort of costumes the lumpy cloth pile represented, and sighed. Anastasia patted her shoulder consolingly.

"Hey, I know it's against the rules, but you can stay up here a while, without me. Take a look at these. Lock the door behind you," Anastasia said, standing and moving towards the door, her glittery crochet shawl fluttering around her shoulders. She paused in the frame, and only turned her head back to say offhandedly, "Harry's having a party this weekend. Saturday night, his place. You should come. It's just crew so far, but he wouldn't mind. I know he likes you. It would do you some good to get out for some fun. Anyway. Look, lock, party. I will see you later." And between one blink and the next, she was gone.

Bella blinked and waved at the suddenly empty doorway, an afterimage of Stasi's eclectic clothing hanging in her gaze. Bella turned her attention to the pile of costumes and sighed.

*     *     *

Some unknown time later, Bella threw aside the last garment the costume master had set aside for her and shook her head at Stasi's idea of *ethereal.* "Strange taste you've got, girl," she muttered, turning from the three-way mirror in her bra and underwear and padding over to the aisles of outfits behind the makeup area.

The musty odor of clothes assailed her nose as she pushed through the crowded aisles, sequins and lamé brushing across her bare arms and legs. The light failed the farther in she walked, the single bulb overhead obscured by hat boxes bearing labels from decades ago and bags of tulle from productions of years past.

Bella stopped when the shadows outnumbered the light, and trailed her fingers along something furry. She took a step forward into a cleared but ill-lit area and stubbed her toe on a loose board. Cursing, she hopped about for a moment until her calves encountered a ledge, and she sat down abruptly. Her fingers traced the outline of what turned out to be a trunk, and found a leather handle above a rusty lock, which yielded to her manipulations with a creak.

Bella could hardly see into the trunk's interior, but her hands encountered silken fabric, and mounds of it. She pulled scarf after scarf from the trunk, throwing them behind her until the air was filled with the diaphanous cloth. The scarves drifted down around her, diffusing the little light available so they almost seemed to glow. Far from being musty, a breath of cinnamon and cloves floated down with the scarves.

She couldn't say what made her dig to the bottom of the chest. When she pulled the last rectangle from the interior, the fabric snagged on a rough edge and tore with a sigh.

"Oh, no," Bella whispered, and followed the ragged fabric to the offending splinter. She lifted the silk from the snag, and gasped when, with a thunk, a piece of trunk's wall slid down, revealing a side compartment.

A grin lit her face as her questing fingers found a thin box hidden in the space. A single scarf, just dislodged from the shoulder of a fur coat by a stray breath of air, settled gently on her back as she sat on her heels and opened the box.

The light seemed brighter with the lid open. Inside was a necklace, a single silver charm on a delicate chain. The charm was shaped like a B, the two loops of the letter reminding Bella of dragonfly wings. In different circumstances, perhaps, Bella would have replaced the necklace in its hiding place and told Anastasia about it. But it was fate, wasn't it, to find something like this, so clearly meant for her? Convinced, she fastened the chain's clasp around her neck.

Instantly, the light changed. It...*sparkled*, somehow. All the dust motes stirred by her passage glimmered in the half-light, and a breath of wind sent shivers across her skin. An incomprehensible voice whispered in her ear, and Bella stood in a rush, grabbing a hunk of silken scarves. She ran back the way she came, the air around her swirling in visible, glittering waves.

At first, the three-way mirror showed nothing awry. She was still clad in her underwear, her auburn hair just settling around her shoulders. It wasn't until she turned to the side and saw the reflection of her reflection in one of the side mirror panels that she stilled in shock, putting a hand to the mirror as if she could touch what she saw there.

The being staring back at her couldn't possibly be real. Her skin was too white, too shimmering. The hair was too red, the eyes an impossible combination of blue and green. The clump of scarves she clutched in her hands matched the sheer sleeves of the dress draping that ethereal body.

The necklace at her throat flashed in that bizarre mirror image, and Bella took a step back from its unreality. No longer able to see the endlessly repeating reflection, she closed her eyes and exhaled loudly. After a moment of fear, she opened her eyes and saw only herself, and felt a little silly for imagining such things. It was late, and she was tired, and her mind was playing tricks on her.

A few minutes later she had dressed in her street clothes and left the handful of scarves she had carried with her on top of the clothes Anastasia had picked out for her. Perhaps the wardrobe department could make something of them.

It wasn't until she woke up the next morning that she realized she still had on the necklace.

*     *     *

Bella stood on the porch of Harry's house, a small brownstone in Dogtown, wind blowing through leaves lost in darkness. Now that she was here, she wasn't sure she wanted to go in. She felt awkward and not quite invited, however much Stasi thought Harry wouldn't mind. Just as she turned to go back to her car, the door opened. Bella paused, her face scrunched up in embarrassment. She let out a soft sigh at the sight of him silhouetted in the door, his black hair disappearing into the darkness of the hallway, his blue eyes shining in the half-light of the streetlamp.

"Isabella," Harry said softly. "I didn't think you would come." His brogue lilted in her ears.

Bella stared at him for a moment, then blurted, "What?"

Harry looked down at his feet, hands braced on the door jamb. "I asked Stasi if she would ask you," he said. Then he chuckled, and delivered a short bow. "Please come in, my lady."

He straightened and offered his elbow. Bella bit her lip, still unsure, then took his arm with a small smile. His skin was cooler than her own, she noted absently.

"Everyone is in the backyard, under the trees," Harry said, leading her through the house, hardwood floors creaking under their feet. She could see flashes of light ahead, but trees obscured most of the view through the rear windows.

"Close your eyes," Harry said earnestly, and Bella had to comply. He lead her a few steps across a tiled floor and she heard the sound of a screen door opening. The cool evening air brushed along her arms for a moment, then Harry said, "Take a look," the smile evident in his tone.

Bella opened her eyes to a scene out of a fairy tale. Strands of lights wound throughout the trees, wrapped around trunks, dripped from branches. Tiny sconces hung from many trees, their candles shielded from touching the wood. Conversation tables dotted the yard, covered with gauzy tablecloths. Harry pulled Bella forward, his grin infectious. Bella could hardly believe she was still in a suburban home.

After Harry showed her a seat in a circle of chairs, he took a place in the middle, still smiling. "Now that our guest of honor is here," he said, winking at her before showing a mocking grin to his other guests, "do you wish to hear a fairy tale about our good theater, the oldest and largest outdoor theater in the nation?"

Murmurs of appreciation and expectation greeted his question. Anastasia came up behind Bella and knelt next to her to whisper in her ear, "You've not heard Harry's stories yet. He makes technical rehearsals so much more endurable. When you know there's a tale waiting for you at the end of the night, you can get through anything."

Bella grinned in response and settled back in her chair in anticipation. Anastasia seated herself on the ground, legs crossed. Harry paced a small circle and glanced over his shoulder at Bella and Stasi, and just before he turned away, he winked at Bella.

"Our story is set in 1927, when the Municipal Theater produced *The Song of the Flame*. Now," Harry said, with a conspiratorial wink, "this is, after all, a fairy tale. But what I will tell you is true...after a fashion."

The lights in the trees seemed to dim as Harry lowered his voice. "Lily was a newcomer to the theater scene. Always restless in her little rural town, she came to the big city to try her luck the first chance she got. She happened to see an advertisement for chorus members in the Post-Dispatch, and answered it on a whim.

"Little did she know that she was destined for greatness, or so thought the director of the show. He heard her sing and declared he had his leading lady. She performed ably enough, but as time wore on, it was apparent that passion was no substitute for experience. The director exploded, in a quaint 1920's way, of course, and told her that she was in danger of losing her part to the shrub she acted behind, so wooden was her acting. Not so unlike our own Bella," he said, voice gentle, blue eyes catching hers.

She couldn't help the flush that spread over her cheeks at the attention of the entire group. But Harry made it sound like it was just an aside, and continued with his story, drawing the eyes of the crowd from her. "Distraught, she fled to the catwalks and hid there until everyone had left. With the gas lights long since extinguished, the stars were clear and sparkling above the outdoor stage. The moon was new and the night was surprisingly cool for a St. Louis summer, and the fey walked in that darkness. There were still some otherworldly creatures that inhabited the park then, before the city had enclosed it utterly.

"One of these beings heard her cries and saw the tears pooling on the stage, and drew close. Eyes closed, the actress didn't notice that the kindly voice speaking words of comfort was a member of the Fair Folk. She didn't even know what was being said, in truth, but the tone somehow conveyed the meaning. Something was offered, and she accepted without thinking. A cold weight settled against her chest, and she looked down to see a silver necklace dangling a delicate charm around her throat. *For luck*, she heard whispered in her head, and she nodded, acquiescing, taking whatever help she could get."

Bella put a hand to her throat, feeling the cool lump of metal hidden under her shirt. She hadn't taken it off except to shower since she found it at rehearsal, somehow feeling more comfortable in her skin with it circling her neck. It *was* silver, and the charm *was* delicate, but quickly dismissed that line of thought. It was too absurd.

Harry continued his story. "Lily awoke the next morning back home in her bed, and thought it all a dream. But the necklace still circled her throat, and she felt a new-found confidence in her ability. She went to the next rehearsal and the next, and the director had no cause to call her out. She surprised everyone with her acting, and her singing made even the comedic chants sound melodious.

"She heard gossip among her fellow actors about the acting tragedy that had happened in Chicago—a new actress had completely blown her opening night—and paid it no mind until she heard that the actress blamed her fall, depending on the teller, on the loss of an old bracelet, or a set of antique earrings, or a ring of uncertain manufacture, or a necklace..."

Bella gasped, and hoped no one heard. Harry continued, "She was uneasy about the necklace now, an insidious voice in her mind telling her that her talent was easily taken away. But she decided that any help was better than none, and chose not to believe the tales."

Harry paused and made a round about the chairs, weaving through the rapt audience and the trees. The sconces sputtered as he passed. "Opening night came, and she received a standing ovation. And then the next night, and the one after that. All seemed to be going well, and the luck of the necklace seemed to be holding, if that was truly what was causing her progress. But this would not be a fairy tale without a damsel in distress, would it?" he mused, trailing his hand along the back of Bella's chair. She sat very still, caught by the gentle wind of his passage, and the scent of cinnamon and cloves following in his wake.

Harry paused underneath a tree, the flickering sconce shadowing his face strangely, his eyes glittering like blue flame. "The last night of the show, everything happened as normal, and as you all know, being superstitious theater blokes yourself, this would typically foreshadow a perfect closing night. Lily was hopeful that this part might be a springboard for other opportunities, and almost dreaded its end. But she went on stage, confident that something, whether the necklace or beginner's luck, would carry her through.

"The first act went off without a hitch. The audience was at capacity, drawn by the stellar reviews. The night was cool but not chilly, and the stars were bright overhead. Intermission came, and Lily waited backstage for the second act. She sat alone, surrounded by the bustle of crew, and sipped a glass of water. A props man jostled her, catching a few strands of her hair, for which he profusely apologized. She felt oddly distanced from the rest of the players all of a sudden, but the house lights flashed once, twice, and it was time for the show to begin again.

"Far from the smoothness of the first act, Lily felt as though a blanket had been thrown over her, muffling sound and making her movements sluggish. Her lines always seemed to come a moment too late and she knew her voice was not hitting notes cleanly. She finished the show, but the bemused glances of the cast and the lukewarm applause from the audience told her how poor the performance had been. The director was waiting for her backstage, but she had no explanation for him, at least not one he would accept."

Harry moved out of the shadows of the trees and entered the circle of chairs again. "It was only when she sat in her dressing room for the last time that she noticed the necklace was gone, lost, perhaps when the crewman bumped into her. Through the fairies' capriciousness or simple bad luck, she had lost her charm and without it, she could not repeat her glorious debut. Oh, she tried, in small shows around the city later in the season, but after that summer, Lily never set foot on a stage again."

Bella sighed with the rest of the listeners, and put a hand to her throat. Harry gave her an odd look, and let the silence stretch for a moment too long. He startled them all with his gravely spoken words. "Perhaps it was the loss of the necklace that caused her fall. Perhaps she deluded herself into thinking that such a trinket could make her something she was not. But know this: you should never let down your guard in places where fantasy is made true, if only for a little while. Let none of you fall into the fey trap of overconfidence! And let all of you step safely through the worlds we create."

Bella could not help but think Harry's story was for her benefit. She saw the disturbed looks on the faces of the people around her, and hunched in her chair. The stage manager saw them too, and once again spun in a lazy circle, meeting each person's eyes. "You wished for a happy ending, did you? The fey will not give you one. They are vindictive and shifty, for immortality can bore them. It is for you to make your destiny. Remember, your life is yours to direct," Harry said. His eyes lit on Bella's, and narrowed as he saw her hand at her throat. He spoke softly, "Not the fey's."

She dropped her hand quickly, turning her gaze to the darkness beyond the twinkling lights in the trees. *He couldn't know, could he?* she thought. *He couldn't think that I have the—*

Shaking her head at the folly of thinking she had found a fairy necklace, she resolutely turned back to face Harry, who was staring at her intently, a strange gleam in his eyes. The shifting lights in the trees cast odd shadows on his face, making it seem lean and angular. Suddenly he was *different*, and she shuddered. He moved towards her, and she stood up abruptly, upsetting her chair.

"I have to go," she said, voice shaking. Barely noticing the astonished faces of the crew, she ran up the steps into the house and then out to her car. She felt Harry's eyes on her back the entire way.

*   *   *

*Hell Week*, they called it. The week before the performance, when every detail mattered and practices ran deep into the night. Tempers were short, words were heated, but the production came together.

When Bella came to the first full dress rehearsal, Anastasia came up to her with a load of fabric in her arms. It was disturbingly familiar, and even more so when Stasi pulled her to a mirror and held an outfit in front of Bella's body.

"Where did you find it, you fiend? I've been through that green room top to bottom before and never noticed anything like it. I would give anything to be able to make something like this. Magical, the fingers that did," she said with a sigh. She drew the fabric to her, stroking the multi-hued silk with envying fingers.

Bella still stood staring at the mirror, her breaths uneven and shallow. It hadn't been a dream, if Stasi was holding that dress, and unless Stasi was hallucinating too, that fabric was real. She clutched at the necklace at her throat and nearly yanked it off, but a wink of light on the mirror made her turn. Sure enough, the three-way mirror reflected the reflection of someone else. Bella knew her expression was stunned, felt the contours of her face constrict in a rictus of fear, but the fey thing in the mirror glared provocatively at her, lips pursed, barely restraining a grin. She was staring at *herself*, of course. But she had never worn that dress, and the shining hair whipped by an unfelt wind was not Bella's auburn.

"--eh? Bella?" Stasi's voice startled her back to reality. Seconds had passed, only. And Stasi was oblivious, chattering in her way. "Where'd you find this?"

Bella gave one last glance to the mirror and let go of the necklace. "It found me," she said softly. Stasi looked at her askance, but let the matter drop.

*       *       *

"What did you *do* over the weekend, Bella?" the director asked, pulling her aside after the rehearsal. "I know...I know I was a little harsh on you last week. But hey, it worked," he said, looking abashed.

"I didn't do anything, sir. Just found a costume." Bella couldn't say any more, couldn't articulate what she felt as she paced the stage, reciting her lines. Nothing had seemed different to her, but she knew from the faces of her fellow actors that they perceived her as someone changed.

"Yeah, that costume. Something else. Stasi find that for you? In our green room? Indeed. Well, keep it up, Bella. I knew I took you on for a reason." He smiled, just a hint of laughter in his eyes. Bella smiled back at him, knowing it was just his way.

She was walking back to the greenroom to store her costume when she encountered Harry. They both stopped and took a step back. Bella couldn't keep her eyes on his, and dropped her gaze.

"You ran away, Bella. Why?" His voice was low, barely audible over the after-rehearsal bustle. Crew and cast eddied around them like water over pebbles in a stream, causing the silk of Bella's dress to flutter around her legs.

"You wouldn't understand." She turned away, crossing her arms.

"What happened to you? It's a story. It had some truth, once. It's an old tale, and I can tell it as feels true." Harry grabbed her arm, pulling her toward him. "Something spooked you. What?"

Bella looked at him, his blue eyes so earnest. Could she tell him? "You said there was some truth. How much?"

"Bella, why are you asking? You're different out there. This outfit...where did you find it? What did you do to your hair? What did you find this past weekend, Bella?" Harry's gaze fell to her throat as she covered the thin chain attached to the dragonfly charm. *"What did you find?"*

He pulled her hand away, prying her fingers from around the charm. "Oh, gods," he whispered, his eyes taking on a frightening glow. "What have you done?"

She frowned at him. "What are you talking about?"

A shout from the catwalk made them both look up. "Raeon, we need you up here. The gels are all mixed up."

Harry glared at his fellow crewman and said, "In a minute. I'm busy."

"Raeon, we need you now. We want to go home," came the voice from above.

Grimacing, Harry slapped the stair rail, and the entire structure clanked. "We need to talk about this, and soon, *caraid*," he said, and ran up the spiral staircase to the catwalk.

*     *     *

Bella often biked home from rehearsals as her apartment was only a few blocks from Forest Park. The streetlights along Lindell were never burnt out or broken, the trees making a chiaroscuro of the sidewalk. She had a can of pepper spray attached to her key fob, just in case. Million-dollar houses faced the park, set far back from the road. She often wondered if the people silhouetted in the well-lit windows would come to her aid if she needed it, or if they would even notice the commotion outside their immaculately-manicured lots.

The rehearsal had gone late tonight, which wasn't unusual for the week before the performance. Most of the windows were dark, porch lights only lighting parts of the lawn. The brisk wind at her back propelled her forward, but raked the tree branches across the lights, checkering the sidewalk. Bella pedaled hard, eager to be home, trying to ignore the eerie similarity to the shadows created at Harry's party.

When she did get home and prepared for bed, she found she couldn't sleep. Harry's strange words kept circling in her head. What had she found? A necklace. What's so wrong with that? It matched the outfit, after all. She must have just not noticed the dress hidden among all the scarves. What had she done? Used a prop, one that might resemble something in a story that might have some truth to it.

*That, and I keep seeing the wrong person in the mirror,* she thought. It had to be some trick of lighting, of strategically placed gels. *A trick that only shows up when I see a reflection of my reflection...*

Sleep caught her then, and she dreamed of the theater, and Harry. She stood on the catwalk of the Muny and trailed her fingers along the edge. A larger hand covered hers, and she looked up into Harry's intensely blue eyes. Shadows obscured his face, and his voice, when he spoke, was deeper, more inflected with his husky accent.

*"Do you know what you have done,* mo chridhe*?"* he said, the words resonating among the leaves of the trees growing through the floor of the stage, making them shiver, making her shiver. *"It will not be worth what you will lose."*

The world went white, and she woke up to the blinding light of day.

*       *       *

Bella struggled through work the next day, and the next. She couldn't focus, couldn't keep from thinking about the oddity that was her life. Mechanically, she did her job, managing to meet her deadlines, but her mind was elsewhere.

The cast had a break after the first dress rehearsal; the crew needed a technical run-through. Tonight, then, she would be back on stage, put on that costume, say her lines, and become someone else. And Harry...she was going to avoid Harry as much as she could. Having him show up in her dreams was too weird, she thought, then laughed. As if a boy being a part of her dream could top the incongruity of her reflection.

Her stomach was in knots as she rolled her bike to the backstage area and locked it up. This rehearsal would check the blocking progress for the first act, with an abbreviated technical crew providing main character spots and musical cues only. Tomorrow would be the same, but for the second act. So there was no reason why she should feel this nervous, right?

When it was time to take the stage, her costume seemed to move of its own volition as she went through the choreography. It fluttered in a non-existent wind no one else could feel. The spotlight was blinding, but instead of sweating under the lights and the ever-present summer humidity, Bella felt cold. Her hands were white under the spot's illumination, but she told herself it was just an illusion. She clutched the silver charm, knowing its metallic chill, at least, was real.

She was sure the director would come up to her afterwards, perfect costume and all, because she knew her acting had been poor. But no one was waiting for her in the wings, and faster than she thought possible, the backstage area emptied of all people. Except for Harry.

Bella nearly tripped over her own feet when she heard him speak her name. She could barely see him, half-hidden in the shadows as he was. Only his eyes gave him away, eyes that seemed to burn in the darkness.

"You were glowing out there, *mo chridhe*. And not just under the spot." He moved further from the light, but she could still see his outline. His body was silver-limned; his skin was pale, but this was no ordinary sheen.

"You glow like I do. You command the stage without trying. I did not tell that story because of you, but fate will have her way. Be careful what you put your faith in," Harry said, his lilting voice trailing off into echoes. Between one blink and the next, his faint outline was gone, and Bella was once again not sure if she had imagined the entire thing.

*       *       *

Bella didn't see Harry the entire next day. She heard his name bandied about and imagined him standing behind the giant spotlight that would illuminate her over the heads of the audience, his blue eyes boring into her. She touched the necklace frequently, taking comfort in its coolness. A part of her was detached, chronicling the moments when she knew she faltered, yet no one remarked on it. When she missed a step once, the director swooped in for what she was sure would be a rebuke, but instead it was to commend her for finding a new way to express the point of the scene.

At the end of the night, the director announced there would be no rehearsal the next day, since everything was going so well. Sunday they would run through the show as many times as was needed. Bella sighed with relief, hoping a day off would calm her subconscious and let her sleep without dreaming. She left the stage in a rush, not wanting to talk to anyone, ignoring the stares--some awed, some jealous--as she passed.

*     *     *

Just outside the Muny, she stopped short, looking across the valet parking area to the gazebo. It stood on an island in the middle of a small lake, filled with ducks and geese and water-skating insects in the daylight. But in the late hour, so late that all the lights had been turned off, all she could see was the amber winking of fireflies and two pinpoints of blue in a silver aura seeming to float at the gazebo's apex.

"Are you watching me, Harry?" she whispered into the night.

She hadn't expected an answer, but wasn't altogether surprised when she had one. "Indeed, *mo chridhe*. For your own good."

*     *     *

Bella woke up on Sunday after a dream of that reflected self dancing madly with Harry in a moonlit sylvan glade. She had slept with the necklace on, and moved to take it off, frightened by the intensity of her subconscious imaginings. A small, superstitious voice suggested that she would need all the help she could get to keep performing as she had. She let her hand drop.

When she arrived at the Muny that afternoon, she stood at the foot of the green room stairs, staring out at the stage. Props had strung garlands of silk vines from the catwalk, integrating them with the living trees that formed the back wall of the stage. She had a moment of deja vu, seeing not the fully dressed stage but the wood of her dream the past night. She blinked, and the stage resolved itself to painted silken mimicry.

Bella's eyes followed the path of a particularly long vine to its anchorage in the catwalk. She saw Harry perched at its terminus like a gargoyle, if a handsome one. His black curls hid his eyes, but she knew they were directed her way. He nodded his sun-haloed head, and she looked away, making sure the charm was tucked inside her shirt.

Stasi was waiting for her in the green room, once again admiring the unusual costume. "I just don't know where you found it. When I look at it, it seems like I've seen parts of it before. It teases me, Bella, like a dream I can't remember."

"Don't try," Bella said softly.

*　　*　　*

Once she was on stage, Bella found all her troubles left her, and she was only her character. Out of the corner of her eye she could see the forest that, for everyone else, was only plywood and paint. Lights came up like the sun, but only if her head was turned. The rushing sound of a waterfall was just audible over the whoosh of the huge fans in the auditorium. Her fellow actors were in perfect unison, when she was front and center.

The rehearsal went so well the director was more than happy to call it early. "Go home and get a good night's sleep, everyone. Call tomorrow is 5 pm. Opening night, people! This is going to be a great show. I expect the best from you, and I know I'll get it, after this."

In the long days of summer, the sun was still up as she walked out of the backstage area, rolling her bike beside her. She cast a glance at the gazebo but a noise from the recessed ticket booth made her turn. Harry waited in the shadows, arms crossed. His outline shimmered, barely visible in the ruddy evening glow. "I wondered if I'd see you in the sunlight," she said, idly.

"It's cooler here, *mo chridhe*," he said. "But you have the right of it, night is more my time." He pushed himself off the wall and reached out to take her hand. "Bella, you have to listen to me. I've seen what's happening to you. It will take you over, if you let it, and you are not resisting."

She looked at him sidelong as they walked towards the parking lot. "And how do you know that?"

He frowned, and ran his hand through his hair. "I know what they're capable of, Bella."

"Ah, *they*. Who's *they*, and what are they capable of?"

"The fey, Bella. The Fair Folk...my people."

Luckily they had just crossed the bridge over the gazebo lake, and a bench was handy, because Bella's legs didn't seem to work at that moment. His words made no sense, but she had seen his eyes burn in the darkness. All she could choke out was, "You're a fairy?"

Harry sighed and sat next to her, steadying the bike she had forgotten about. "I prefer 'fey,' Bella. I don't have wings or carry a wand. But legend nonetheless," he said, his accent stronger with emotion. "I tell you this because that trinket you wear is of our make. I did not know you had it when I told that story, but as I've said, fate will have her way, and perhaps it was meant as a warning. But you've not heeded it. They gave it, and will take it as suits them, certainly not as it suits you."

"Like magic," Bella said faintly. "So you enjoy making a laughingstock of us humans?"

"I have been here long enough that I do not look down on you. Unless I'm on the catwalk, of course," he amended with a smile. "I saw you from up there, glowing like one of our own. Bella, it's a glamour only. A powerful one, to be sure, but illusion! If you suddenly find yourself without it, would you be able to carry on?"

"You don't think I could?" she asked with a bit of heat.

"I know you could, *mo chridhe*, and that is the point. You do not need it. Will you try?"

"What if I can't do it? Take it off?" *What if I don't want to?*

He took her hand. "It is your choice, Bella." He stood up, silhouetted in the setting sun. "I, for one, will not look for your downfall." He took a step away and smiled at her, blue eyes flashing. Then he grinned, snapped his fingers, and disappeared.

*     *     *

*Remarkable aplomb, that's what I have,* Bella thought to herself as she walked backstage. Standing on the apron, she took a last look at the empty, open-air auditorium and sighed. Soon those seats would be filled and none of them would believe this production had a member of the Fair Folk as its stage manager, or that the lead actress was laboring under an illusion...

Stasi was waiting for her in the wings, all the costumes carefully labeled and hung up in order of use. Stasi held up Bella's as she passed, and said, "Break a leg, sweetheart."

Bella gave her a small smile and held the small box, containing an innocent-looking silver necklace, closer to her chest.

*     *     *

Harry caught her just before she reached the wings, at the five-minute call. "You are being awfully trusting tonight," he said, nodding towards the necklace she had donned just moments before.

"It's opening night. I took it off during the day, but I...I need it now. Everything works when I wear it, not just me. It might be illusion but it's a damn good one, and what is acting but making people believe something is true that isn't?"

He shook his head, the radiance about him intensifying for a moment in the dim hallway. "You have no need of this, Bella," he said, putting his hand over the charm. "You are more than it makes you, no matter what you think, and it is *holding you back*," he said harshly, clenching the charm in his fist and yanking it away.

Bella took a step back from his unexpected violence. "Why did you *do* that?"

"For your own good, *mo chridhe*. Find your strength in another way. They would take it from you, my people, and take it in the worst way possible. Now you know you stand on your own, without trickery. Hate me if you must, but if you wear this tonight, you will forever wonder if it was your talent that drove the show, or theirs."

Harry stepped back into the shadows, his outline faded to nothing. Bella stared after him with something close to despair, and it was only routine that rescued her as the overture started to play, and she took her place on stage.

$*$        $*$        $*$

Bella felt like her head had been wrapped in wool as she went through the first act. The ease of the past week's rehearsals was gone, replaced by memorized steps. Her fellow players frowned at her as they left the stage, and every time she moved off to the wings, she had to tilt her face towards the newly-appeared stars to keep from crying.

Halfway through the act, she happened to look up at the catwalk and saw Harry crouched by a light. He smiled at her and blew her a kiss, and Bella felt it on her brow as if he had actually laid it there. Her smile, when she returned it, was tremulous but real, and she walked out to deliver her next lines with renewed spirit.

Finally the curtain closed for intermission, and Bella ignored everyone as she ran to her dressing room. When the knock sounded at her door, somehow she knew it was Harry even before she heard his distinctive tenor. "Come in," she called.

"Bella, *mo chridhe*, you are stronger than this small magic," he said softly as he entered, dangling the necklace from his fingers. Bella watched him in the mirror, closing her eyes briefly as his hands settled on her shoulders. "You have a story of an elephant that can fly by aid of a feather," he said, stroking her arms through the silk. "That feather was lost, and he learned to fly without it, and better than before. As can you. Your destiny is more glorious than glamour can ever make it."

Harry held the charm in front of them both. Without breaking gaze with Bella in the mirror, he palmed it, then spread his fingers to show it had disappeared. He bent his head to hers, his eyes asking permission. Bella turned her face to his. "I believe in you, *mo chridhe*," he said, then kissed her.

Bella smiled against his lips. "What was that for, Raeon?"

He grinned back at her, his aura brightening around both of them. "For strength of a different kind."

# Leaving my Life in St. Louis

By P. Anthony Mast

As I drive into St. Louis, crossing over the mighty, muddy Mississippi River, I glance in the rearview mirror and catch a glimpse of the box in the back seat of my car. It holds my dead wife and son.

I fight back the tears once again. The trip from Virginia to St. Louis has been a long one. But after fourteen hours of driving, I am finally within sight of my final destination.

I glance toward the Arch. After being away for a few years, I am awed by its splendor. It is a marvel and gives the town its unique skyline. I roll my eyes. I'm starting to sound just like the travel guide I studied when I started planning this trip. I keep my gaze from falling farther north, where I am ultimately headed.

When I last lived in St. Louis, the Eads Bridge was used only for the new light rail system which connected the northwest end of town at the Airport to just east of town on the Illinois side of the river. Now the bridge has a newly paved topside and accommodates both vehicle and foot traffic. Though, from the way Anna's mom talks, the only uses for it are the summer festivals.

Anna…

She was my wife. We met in high school, though never knew each other as more than casual acquaintances. A ten-year reunion brought us from opposite coasts to the western edge of St. Louis. I remember joking with her about how little the significance of "Where'd you go to high school?" seemed to have in DC and Seattle. You can tell so much about someone from St. Louis by the school they attended. Try as I might to distract myself with a wandering thought, I can't push my memories past the last few days… to remember how we met again… how I proposed… I can't remember our wedding day… how she looked in the dress. I can't remember anything except seeing what was left of her, broken and charred, cradling our son... I can't remember either of their faces.

Danny...

My baby boy was only two and a half years old when he was taken from me. The fire started in a neighboring apartment. I stepped out of the apartment for only twenty minutes... I ran to get a pack of cigarettes... still haven't smoked one of them. I came back to see the top two floors of the building in flames. I was sure when it was just the top two floors that Anna and Danny had made it out. I tore through the crowd of neighbors. I couldn't find Anna and Danny.

I didn't know at that moment Danny was already gone and Anna was either dead or cradling the body of our dead son. The firefighters told me she wrapped herself around him when she found him. I still don't understand how they could tell. Maybe they just told me that to make me feel better. She made no attempt to save herself as the smoke engulfed the apartment.

My honey, my sweetheart, was gone. My buddy, my angel, was taken with her.

Our friends and family attended the memorial; I don't remember the service.

Her mom talked me into cremation. I didn't care. They were gone. She could do whatever the hell she wanted with the corpses. Those two blackened bodies with cloth burnt to the charred flesh weren't my wife and son... my wife and son had left. They left without saying goodbye and left without a way for me to follow or find them.

I drive for a while without realizing exactly where I am, and where I am heading. I suppose I must have passed the new Busch Stadium. Even on the East Coast, we had Danny in Cardinals hats and t-shirts when those around us dressed their kids in Nationals gear.

Muscle memory guides me along the twists and turns of Highway 40 through the heart of St. Louis. I barely notice passing the hockey arena, Union Station, Forest Park and all of the attractions which go along with it...

I return to a more conscious place in my driving as I approach and guide the car onto Interstate 170, the north-south corridor connecting the middle and northern areas of St. Louis County.

There will only be another 10 minutes before I enter the home of Jean and John Scarvin, my wife's parents. They were never really crazy about me, but look as if I bear the Holy Grail when I stumble into their home just a few minutes past 10:00 PM and hand them the matching urns containing what was once my wife and son.

I know what they think of me and don't give a damn. They look at the metal containers the same way they looked at Anna and Danny when they came to visit. They think the bodies, now ashes, are their only connection to their daughter and grandson. I suppose I really shouldn't fault them. It must be what keeps them sane through this insane time. And oddly enough, the three of us for the first time in a long time have something in common; we all lost Anna, and we all lost our only child.

I have all of my wife and son I could hope to have under the circumstances. The laptop holding backups of all of our pictures had been in the car the night of the fire. Anna also kept a blog. Her internet diary catalogued everything she and Danny did each day. She kept it as much for herself and for us as she did for her parents. I have those things. I have an old Def Leppard concert t-shirt. Anna wore it to bed at least once a week since we were married. I have the turtle blanket, a little blanket with the plastic upper body of a turtle Danny used when he was teething and slept with every night. It was in his bedroom... the only room spared from the flames but destroyed by water and debris when the ceiling caved in on the room a few hours after the blaze started.

The shirt, the blanket and a few bytes on a computer, my whole life was wrapped up in these few things.

I say goodbye to John and Jean, and they are as civil to me as they were on the day I took their daughter east. They don't understand how I can leave Anna and Danny with them. They don't try too hard though, not when it means they will be the keepers of the ashes.

I leave the house and walk back to the car. My gaze falls on the back seat where indentations mark the fabric where Danny's car seat had once been. My body retches violently. It is the only way my body reacts anymore. The tears are a constant, but the only real outward reactions I have are the violent releases of whatever is in my stomach when I think of my baby boy. I hadn't had more than water and a few chips in the past few days, so this bout is, in relation, minor.

It is only a few minutes before I drive back onto the highway. At this hour, the best bet to find a hotel room is near the airport. Money isn't a concern. The estate will take care of the credit card bills.

While driving north on Interstate 170 toward Lambert International Airport, I pick up my cell phone from the seat next to me. I stopped for lunch at a café in Pennsylvania. While there I looked up the numbers for a few hotel chains and enter the numbers into the phone's memory. I never intended on staying with her parents, and shouldn't be surprised they didn't even offer a bed.

With the Boy Scout motto of "Be Prepared" and a few phone calls while turning onto Interstate 70, I secure a room for the night before reaching the hotel.

The night clerk is a sympathetic looking girl who speaks broken English. I know enough to presume she is from Eastern Europe, but the exact accent is beyond me. St. Louis has become one of the cities experiencing a rise in immigrant population from Croatia, Slovakia, and a few of the other Eastern Bloc countries still trying to fend for themselves in the new world market.

I am thankful for her lack of ability to get the words out quick enough to ask me what is wrong. I don't know if the poor girl could handle some guy walking in and doubling over with a bout of dry heaves.

I take a quick detour through the closed bar. I drop a fifty-dollar bill to ease my conscience for taking a half full bottle of Dalmore Scotch and a full can of Planter's Mixed Nuts.

I ride the elevator to the eighth floor and traverse the halls until I find the door to my room.

With the swipe of an electronic key card, the lock clicks and buzzes. I push my way into my room. I drop the duffle bag on the floor by the bathroom and strip out of my shirt while kicking off my shoes.

I walk to the table which holds the tray with two bags of instant coffee, two glasses with little paper caps and an ice bucket with a plastic bag hanging out of it. I pull one of the glasses from the tray, flick the paper covering off with my thumb, and place it next to the bottle of whiskey. With no resistance, the cork stopper slides off with a slight pop of displaced air. I pour the yellow-amber liquid until the glass is half full, and then replace the stopper.

I find my way to the chair, the same semi-comfortable chair occupying every hotel room. I push it over to the window, open the curtain, and sit back into the chair. I have a glass of whiskey in my right hand, the turtle blanket in my left and the old, black, concert t-shirt crumpled in my lap.

Danny loved watching airplanes. We would run around the house with him under my arm, his arms outstretched, making jet engine sounds as we flew from the hidden base in his room, through the enemy territory of the living room. The mission would end when my arms got tired and we took a dive bomb into Mommy Mountain. Anna woke this same way every Saturday and Sunday morning for the past year and a half. It was Friday night. Anna wasn't going to wake up again, and Danny wasn't going to be an airplane, flying with my help through our apartment.

I sit and watch the airplanes take off and land all night long.

I don't recall falling asleep, but I also don't remember dawn breaking. Sleep must have gently accepted me at some point in the night and had been merciful enough to deny me dreams.

I stand from the chair, still clutching the blanket and t-shirt. At some point before dawn, I placed the untouched whiskey on the floor.

I place the relics of my family on the untouched bed. Even in this strange place, I let my body take over and go through all of the motions of my morning rituals. I stop cold as I stand over the toilet. I almost collapse at the memory of Danny running through the apartment naked from the waist down shouting, "Daddy! I pee-pee standing up. I'm big boy."

These little miracles and milestones are now just memories, and it would be one of the last hurdles Danny ever crossed.

I let the rituals take over and only bring my consciousness to the forefront when I clear the room of my things and check out of the hotel.

When I get to the car, I sit for a few long moments pondering my next stop. I know my tour will end at the Eads Bridge. I consider whether I should take the scenic route and take a trip down memory lane on my way to the highway to Hell, or if I should just head down to the Bridge over Troubled Waters. I can almost feel Anna punching my upper arm for making such a cheesy reference.

I lay my head back against the headrest and let a fresh flood of memories wash over me. I have as little control of when the memories hit me as how I will react to them.

*       *       *

"It? It?!"

My arm stung with the flared knuckle punch Anna had only moments before delivered to my upper right arm. Daniel, without a doubt, taught her that particular attack. Her uncle had been the source of many of Anna's bad habits. She was raised as a prim and proper young lady. And I'm pretty sure the girls in her private grade school hadn't taught her about cocking the knuckle to get the maximum impact when delivering a shot to the upper arm.

"Yeah, it. I mean, it's not like we know if it's going to be a boy or a girl yet." The retort was valid in the logical sense, but it probably wasn't the best idea to goad a pregnant woman.

"It is our baby! IT is not an IT!" Her voice cracked with the inflection of each usage of the word, instantly adding "It" to Anna's personal lexicon of curse words. Tears welled in her eyes and before I could backpedal out of the double slip, those tears flowed along her cheeks and gathered below her chin.

"Honey, you're right. I'm sorry. What color should the paint be for his or her room?" I asked the question again, in what I hoped would be a less offensive way.

"If you would just let me find out, then we could make it special for HIS or HER room."

"Now, let's not have this particular discussion again. We said at the beginning, if one of us doesn't want to know, then we don't find out. And I want it to be a surprise, at least for the first one."

Anna smiled through the tears at the mention of possibly having more children. She wanted at least two.

*     *     *

The memory flees as quickly as it came upon me. I try to focus on Anna's tear-streaked face, but it too fades into vapor and crawls back into my head.

I blink twice to push the tears from my eyes and force them outward toward my cheeks.

I start the car and pull out of the hotel parking lot.

I make my way to Interstate 70 and head east, toward downtown St. Louis.

It is early on Saturday morning and the regular constricted flow of traffic approaching downtown is non-existent.

It doesn't take long to get to the Broadway exit and find a space in the parking garage attached to the grounds of the St. Louis Arch. It took me hours to drive to this city, my mind grinding the whole time, open wide to any and all memories of Anna and Danny I would be lucky enough to pull into my consciousness. The day-long drive seemed to last a week. Every mile brought forth another memory, and each of those memories twisted around in my mind to replay whole conversations, whole days in a matter of minutes.

As my journey approaches its destination, I can't focus enough to find any of those memories. The miles slipped past and in what seemed only a few seconds since I started the car near the airport. I walk out of the garage and up the hill along the bridge.

The sounds of the city surround me and I notice things I hadn't in those times when I would haunt the Laclede's Landing area of St. Louis. The ground rumbles beneath my feet and I feel my body tense. It takes only a moment to remember that to my right, through a few feet of concrete and brick lay the Metrolink. St. Louis' light rail train system has cars which pass to and from the Illinois side of the river. Even at this distance, I can hear the river slapping against the brick supports of the bridge or the asphalt that leads into the water, or perhaps it is a barge just out of view. Each car and truck from the nearby highways proves the Doppler Effect as it relates to sounds approaching and retreating from a point.

I can't focus on any of these, but can't drag my attention from all of them, and something keeps me from remembering on the only thing I want to.

I reach the top of the hill where Washington Avenue leads into the Landing and serves as the entrance to one of the three bridges in the vicinity of downtown St. Louis.

I have the turtle blanket in my left hand and the Def Leppard t-shirt in my right. Even at this early hour, the humidity combined with the warmth should be uncomfortable; instead I feel an incredible chill run through my body as I round in a U-Turn to step up onto the bridge complex.

I feel an emptiness filling me. No, that's not quite right. I feel as though I step outside of myself, like an avatar in one of those 3-D high definition computer games. I watch myself from behind and merely control this body moving along the walkway spanning the bridge. This disembodied experience keeps me from noticing anything in front of me. In an instant, I feel myself pull back into my body. A firm hand grabs my left arm and spins me to face a weasel-faced security guard.

The sudden return to self makes me aware of my senses and the stench of cigarettes and coffee assaults me during the berating from the rent-a-cop.

The bridge is closed. Apparently there had been a few drunken brawls the night before and the vendors didn't want anyone trashing their booths over night. While it isn't night and the bridge is supposed to be open to the public, there is no getting around this wanna-be Barney Fife. I suppose I could deck the bastard and just go to the center span to complete my quest, but if "Andy" is hiding somewhere, he won't take too kindly to me flooring Barney and the real police will be called in.

While I am resolute in my ultimate act of self-destruction, I'm not prepared to get arrested and spend a few days under a suicide watch.

I turn and walk away from the security guard. Behind me he threatens to call the police if I return before the gates officially open for the day.

I find my way down to Lenore K. Sullivan Blvd. This road, named after a politician who died when I was in high school, runs between the St. Louis riverfront and the grounds of the Gateway Arch. Even at this early hour, tourists mill around the levee grounds and make their way to the massive stairway leading up to the Arch.

I ponder taking the trip up to the top, but it seems silly. After all, if I can't open the window at the top. . .

I turn at the end of the levee wall and walk up the stairway leading back to the parking garage.

I find my car and fall back in, placing the relics on the seat next to me. I pull the note from the dash and slip it under the items next to me.

The note is simple and to the point. It gives information about who I was and information about the lawyers to contact to inform of my death. The lawyer has instructions for my remains, if they find them, and how to disperse the money left in my accounts once they have confirmation. The firefighters will get a portion of it, and the rest will go to accounts set up for the other families displaced by the apartment fire.

I drive out of the garage and find my way back to Interstate 64. The folks in St. Louis still can't get past calling it Highway 40, even though it has also been I-64 for at least as long as I've been driving. I head west out of downtown and pull off into the Park.

Forest Park is a huge expanse serving a variety of purposes for the community. It houses the St. Louis Zoo, a planetarium (which spans Highway 40 in the form of the St. Louis Science Center), an outdoor amphitheater, a paddle-boat lake, biking and jogging paths, museums and a number of sporting fields. I drive just past the zoo and cut across the highway to a small parking lot facing the highway and the zoo's parking lot beyond. Parking there is free, but the real attraction is something I always wanted to share with Danny. Turtle Park.

Seven sculpted turtles and a half-dozen eggs make up the playground known as Turtle Park. Children are encouraged to climb on and play around the concrete figures. The area is surrounded by a sculpted snake which provides seating and a barrier between the park and a patch of grass leading to the highway.

My chest tightens as I step out of the car and walk into the still, empty playground. I climb on the back of one of the larger turtles and lay on its back. I look up at the blue sky, watching as a cloud creeps from west to east.

The memories flood through me as tears slide along my cheeks and dampen the turtle beneath me.

"Daddy?"

"Yeah, buddy?"

"Who built the sky?"

What to tell him? Do I try to explain God, and religion, and church, and faith? All of the things we had not shared with our little boy. Do I try to explain that the sky, the atmosphere, is gas trapped by the gravity of the Earth when the solar system formed? How do I teach him without confusing him?

We were lying together on the roof of the apartment building. The three of us relaxed after an afternoon of playing in Danny's inflatable pool.

"Yeah, Daddy. Who made the sky?" I could hear the smirk in Anna's voice without taking my eyes from a slow moving cloud Danny had already determined looked like Nemo. Of the dozen or so clouds we bothered to identify, we had nearly equal distribution of Nemo, Superman and Dorothy the Dinosaur. Anna knew I was pondering it, but wore a wicked grin, gleeful the question didn't fall on her shoulders.

I decided to respond in the only way I could. "Who do you think built the sky, Danny?"

I turned my head to look over at my son as he crooked his head, and scratched his chin in the way he had seen characters on TV when they pondered a decision. "Superman," he finally announced. I never confirmed nor denied the involvement by the Last Son of Krypton in the creation of the sky, and didn't need to as Danny was satisfied enough by his own answer.

Just past him, my wife popped her head up to look at me from the other side of Danny. "Cheater," I read the word on her unspeaking lips.

A sharp jab to my ribs wakes me.

"Come on, pal. Sleep off your partying somewhere else."

My eyes flitter open and I look at the scowling face of a police officer.

"Come on, bud. If you get out of here now I don't have to haul you away in front of the kids. You been drinking?"

"No… um… no, sir. I… My son died five days ago. I… I hoped to bring him here someday…" I feel as if I am sobbing through my words, but it must not be as bad as it seems in my own head.

"I'm sorry. Look, take a few minutes to get yourself together, I'll keep the kids out of the park for a few more minutes, but anything longer and people… well, you know how bad a pushy mom can be." The officer must be trying to lighten the mood. He can't know my son's pushy mom is just a grouping of ashes, too little really even to be called a pile.

"Thanks," I choke the word out. It takes only a moment or two before I compose myself, slide down from the back of the turtle and make my way to the car. On my way past the officer, he tips his cap to me and begins to allow families into the park. Families. Complete families. Moms. Kids.

"Why?!" I scream to no one in particular and slam my fists hard against the upper handle of the steering wheel.

It is a ridiculous question. There is no answer. And if there is one, I'm not an important enough part of the equation to be let in on the cosmic formula that requires the death of a mother and her young son.

I let the tears flow down my cheeks as I drive back to the highway. The roads are only slightly more congested, as I head east.

The bridge should be opening soon. I am tired. I had actually slept without interruption last night, but still… I am tired of living. There is nothing left for me. The love of my life turned to dust. My baby boy, burned away into nothingness.

I turn south off the highway just before crossing the bridge back to Illinois. I am immediately struck by the changes that have happened to the ramps and the roads surrounding the new Busch Stadium. Roads once familiar are either vastly different or non-existent. I navigate by street signs, first finding 8th Street, then cutting over to Broadway as I continue to head south of downtown St. Louis to the Soulard neighborhood.

Soulard is known for its huge Mardi Gras celebrations. It is the location for the headquarters of Anheuser-Busch. In a word association game, when the word is 'Soulard', almost everyone in St. Louis will answer 'Farmer's Market'. Dad used to take me to the Market every Sunday after Mass to gather fresh fruits and vegetables for the week, along with the occasional fresh cuts of meat for Sunday grilling on those nights Mom didn't feel like preparing a big dinner.

I park near the market and open the door to the sights, sounds, and smells that haven't changed in the thirty years since Dad and I came here.

As crazy as it seems, I feel comfort walking through the noise and chaos of the crowded market.

I hoped all of the Sundays spent here would bring back some memory of my father that would ease the ache.

Dad is gone. His ghost is no easier to summon than Anna's or Danny's.

I walk past the stands of fruit, clothing, and vegetables. Nothing I see or hear or smell sparks a memory. I walk toward the exit. Just as I step out of the market, it comes. An unexpected memory.

"So, you going to buy that pretty girl some fruit? Maybe take her to the park? It's a beautiful day," the fruit seller's spoke in a thick, Eastern European accent.

"I don't know. We have a wedding to go tonight, but…"

We came back to St. Louis for the wedding of a mutual friend. Anna had moved to the East Coast six months prior. It had been over a year since the reunion.

"A wedding, eh? Beautiful thing. Nothing like it. Guess it is not your wedding. She wears no ring. Beautiful day, beautiful girl, beautiful fruit, beautiful ring. No way she will turn you down." The man chuckled to himself and cocked his head, looking back and forth between Anna and me.

I laughed. "What if I'm not sure that she's the one?"

"How long you been with her? Must be a while now. You are too comfortable to let a pretty girl like that walk off on her own without you."

"Fourteen months." We had only been in the same city for six months. Fourteen months, saying the number made me realize just how long we had been together. "And besides, I'm not sure if she's the one."

"Fourteen months and you cannot decide? And when you do, when you decide, then you will ask and it will be done then." The man had a look as if he was suspicious of me, or perhaps just studying me.

"Of course."

"You have no bags, you've been here for quite a while, you will buy something, but you are going to wait until just before you leave."

"Yeah…" This old man started to make me anxious. It wasn't that he was threatening or accusatory; he was speaking matter of factly.

"You make a decision. You stick with it. But until you are ready, you don't decide. That about right?"

I felt my eyes close to slits. "What's your point?"

"No point, boy. Just noticing a fellow soul." He looked past me to Anna. "Now that is a decision you should make."

The memory fled.

I turn back into the Market and move quickly to the section I remembered him being in. It had been a few years since I had met him, but now I recall the conversation we carried on for almost an hour while Anna worked her way from shop to shop. Adem told me how he left Bosnia in the 90s and made the decision to never return. The country was no longer the one he grew up in and he was happy living here in the United States. There was a good chance Adem was here, and just seeing a familiar face might be something to help me spark more memories from that day.

I remember the day. I can't forget it. It was the day I proposed to Anna, but remembering the day and reliving the memories were proving to be completely different creatures for me these days.

I turn the corner at the back of the market to the leg of the market where Adem should be. His booth is there but I don't see the old man. As I approach the stand, a woman who looks as if she is about my age rises from behind the stand and comes out to greet me.

"Can I do something to help you?" Her accent is similar to Adem's, and, as well as I can remember the fruit seller, she also shares features with him.

"Yes. Ok, this is going to sound bizarre, but… there was a man who worked here."

"Nothing bizarre about that, sir."

"No, I mean… yeah… OK, but this man, Adem. Is this his stand?"

"No. Well, if you ask him it is, but really I think he only says that when my mother is not around." She smiles and I notice her beauty for the first time.

"Is Adem your father?"

"He is. How do you know him?"

"He helped me through a moment of doubt. I wanted to thank him and tell him good bye."

"I can pass that on to him if you would like. He won't be back 'til next week. But if you tell me who you are, I can relay any message to him when they get back from Bosnia."

I thank her for her time and help, and buy a fresh plum. I walk back to the car with my purchase and fall into my seat. I take a few minutes to eat the sweet fruit while trying to keep the sticky, sweet juices inside from ending up all over me.

While walking around the market I noticed a large number of people wearing the familiar Cardinal red. It must be game day today.

I finish the plum, depositing the pit into the bag I used to carry it. I pull out of my parking spot and find my way to Seventh Street where I turn north toward downtown.

I cut over to Broadway and take a lap around the new stadium. I never could see what was wrong with the old one, but this one looks nice enough from the outside. I drive around it twice and watch the families walking into the stadium. I turn east and head toward the Arch grounds again, and then realize seeing families isn't crippling me. I think of Danny and Anna, but the thoughts are pleasant. The thoughts hadn't been pleasant since their deaths.

Tears well in my eyes and I can barely see the road. My heartbeat drums in my ears drowning out all sound around me. In an instant, I am back as a pair of police cars scream past me through the intersection I am about to cross. My heart races.

*My god, I almost died…*

Do I actually accept they are dead? How can I think of them and not hurt? I close my eyes, knowing the image of them will escape me again, but it doesn't. I can see them clearly. Anna sleeps soundly as the morning light casts her shadow on the far wall and Danny curls up next to her waiting for her to wake, or for me to get conscious enough to stumble to the living room to turn the TV on for him.

I turn onto Memorial Drive following the police vehicles that are already out of sight.

My decision has been made. I won't have to accept their deaths much longer. All I have to do is take a step up and jump out into the river. I can't swim. Never learned. I was hoping to learn when Danny did, but he isn't part of my reality any longer.

I park, set the note and the laptop where they can be found. I collect the t-shirt and blanket and walk out of the parking garage.

The scene now is far different than it had been earlier this morning. A crowd is gathering at the top of the hill leading to the bridge. Some people are waving their friends to hurry as others snap photos with cameras and cell phones.

Just as I reach the top of the hill and turn, a news van followed by an ambulance and two more police vehicles comes to a halt in the area being cleared by the police.

I turn to see a man, barely a man… he looks like a boy. This man-boy is holding a gun to the head of the security guard who had assaulted me with coffee, cigarettes and words earlier.

I slowly work my way through the crowd and push to the front. The shouts are full of profanities. The media have set up cameras in an instant and are already focusing boom microphones on the situation. I feel like I should have been upset, that I'm not going to be able to jump today. This isn't the case, things will clear soon enough.

The security guard looks as if he is going to be sick. He had been held hostage long enough to piss himself and the stains on his shirt from his tears and his sweat rivals the stain on his pants. He is crying for his life.

I look at the man-boy. He has made his decision. I can see it in his eyes. These are the same eyes I had seen in the mirror for the past five days. The gun seems ridiculously large in his hand. I don't know much about guns, but at that range, I imagine the guard's head will explode in a particularly gruesome fashion when this thug pulls the trigger.

The police are moving people back quickly as they position vehicles between the crowds and the situation.

"Put down the weapon!" One of the officers shouts to the thug.

"Shit, man… Shit, man, shit!" The guard kept repeating it, probably to keep from actually doing it.

The kid turns to look behind him as the roar of engines comes from the far end of the bridge. The Illinois State police cut off the only other escape route.

One of the officers steps out from behind the car and places his weapon on the ground. He walks with his hands up, inching closer to the scene. "Just put the gun down and let's talk about this. We can get you back to the station and you can tell us what happened."

The kid swings the gun from the head of his prisoner and points it at the approaching officer. "Yeah right, you are just gonna gun me down the way you shot my brother. You…"

The officer cuts him off, "Your brother shot a cop and was holding a little girl hostage. He didn't give us a choice. You have a decision here. You haven't done that much wrong that we can't…"

"Bullshit! You are full of bullshit! My brother got shot when you should have just arrested him. You killed him, and you are gonna kill me. Well, I'm gonna ki-"

"No. Your brother made the decision that got him killed. And you are headed the same way, but it doesn't have to end up like that. You don't have to end up a killer and another stone for your mother to pick out. Just put the gun down and let the hostage go."

"No way. It's over." He emphasizes his statement by pressing the gun hard into the temple of the security guard.

The kid is dead. He is as dead as…

"It's not over. You've made some bad choices this morning, but don't make the last decision you'll ever make. If you pull that trigger, you will be shot. You will most likely be killed. Now put the gun down before even that choice gets taken out of your hands."

A red dot flits on the hand of the kid, showing him the laser sight is trained on him before the dot moved to his forehead. The kid glances around before his eyes settle on the roof of a building a half block away.

The kid looks the officer in the eye and pitches his weapon to the side, pushing the guard away before putting his hands behind his head and falling to his knees sobbing.

I watch as the officers move the kid into a patrol car and mill around collecting names and interviewing witnesses.

I cast my eyes downward, unable to focus on the items in my hands through the tears falling to the concrete sidewalk.

# About the Authors

Den Dotson –

Den was born and raised in St. Louis. In fact, Den tried moving away from St. Louis once. It lasted four months. Now Den visits other places and comes back here to St. Louis as his home. No promises about the future but for now Den is a man of St. Louis.

Den's family has long been associated with St. Louis. Den's great grandfather was an inventor and was honored as one of the "Veiled Prophets" - if you have to ask who a "Veiled Prophet" is you aren't from St. Louis.

Den was born in the hot muggy summer. Attended Bayless High School (essential information if you are from St. Louis), and received a bachelor's degree from Webster University with dual majors in animation and anatomical illustration (he can draw just about anything) and minors in comparative religion and creative writing. Den's creative writing teacher was one of his heroes Glenn Savan. Glenn was the author of a book whose heart was in St. Louis, White Palace.

Den once asked Glenn if he thought Den showed the talents necessary to be a writer. Glenn asked his own question, "What was your grade in my class?" Den answered, "An A." Glenn's reply, "You were the only one."

Den is a life long fan of the fantastic and the futuristic. His writing reflects these visions. He writes science-fiction and fantasy filled with fully realized characters who think, feel, and breath in a world just five steps away from our own. If you like bone-chilling, hair-raising, thought-provoking stories with a dash of belly-shaking, pants-peeing humor-Den is the writer for you.

The story in this volume is just the start of Den's professional writing career. He has finished a rough draft of his first novel, a science fiction adventure (currently being edited), and he is writing a second, a fantasy set in an imaginary and inventive version of the American Old West. Remember his name. You will be seeing it on the spine of many books to come.

Den lives in South St. Louis County with his lovely wife, Colleen, a brilliant photographer, caterer, designer, artist, editor and first reader of all of his work. He would like to dedicate the story in this book and all his work to her for her never ending support and patient love; one artist to another. He couldn't do any of it without her.

Den and Colleen are the designer and photographer responsible for the cover to this book.

Den can be contacted at:
animateden@mac.com

Joshua Ebling –

Josh has been a storyteller since he could dream. With three nearly completed manuscripts in his back pocket, he's currently hoping his own dreams come true, and fast. Living in the shadows of hundreds of amazing fantasy authors and artists, he one day hopes to sit among the greatest in the industry, and to help others do the same. Currently, he resides in St. Louis, where he plots away all night, and sleeps all day, dreaming of the future, and the nature of things long past into darkness.

Josh also does the occasional (but hopefully soon to be more frequent) movie review on the Fanboy Smackdown podcast, www.fanboysmackdown.com.

Josh can be contacted at:
   aberrantfate@gmail.com

Jane Wallace Reed –

Jane Wallace Reed is an artist, poet and writer. Born in St. Louis, Missouri, she now lives in Lebanon, Illinois. She was raised in the Shaw neighborhood, very near Missouri Botanical Gardens. She was raised with a great love of literature, instilled in her by her parents, at an early age. Her father thought it would be fun for her to memorize Robert W. Service's poem "The Cremation of Sam McGee", which Jane was then able to recite, at the advanced age of four-years-old. Some of the books which her parents read to her included all of Mark Twain's works, along with the L. Frank Baum series, including the Wizard of Oz. Thereafter, her older brother read to her. Because of his selections, she still considers herself an only child. Somewhere, before Jane's eighteenth birthday, she actually began reading on her own.

Jane's education includes a B.A. in English, and M.A. in Theatre from St. Louis University. She spent almost half of her life living in the Washington, D.C. area, with her husband. While there, she studied creative writing at The Writer's Center. She also took writing courses at Georgetown University, adventuring into playwriting for awhile, where she wrote a one-act-play that had a staged reading at the Source Theatre. Jane also studied at George Mason University in Fairfax Virginia, where she found a special love of short-story writing, although she primarily considers herself a poet. She finds that whether short-story, play or poem, she tends to encapsulate her thoughts, incorporating emotions and story line, into vignettes of life. She believes that all art is intertwined, with the pen-on-paper reflecting the colors of life, painting moments with words, and the brush-on-canvas summoning up emotions, and telling stories with what a captured image reflects.

Jane also has a strong interest in genealogy. She believes that we are not only impacted by our immediate environment, but, also, we are the products of the people from whom we descend, carrying on both their triumphs and failures, into our own lives. That is why she chose the poem "Ancestor," as one of her works to be included in this anthology.

Jane can be contacted at:

janewreed@gmail.com

Marqua McGull –

A native of St. Louis, Mo., Marqua McGull(Billingsley) earned a Bachelor of Arts in Political Science from St. Louis University and a Juris Doctorate from Loyola University of Chicago School of Law. After residing and practicing law in Chicago, Illinois and Houston, Texas, she and her family relocated to St. Louis, Missouri. Affiliated with The Smith Partnership, P.C. in St. Louis, Mo., she practices law in Illinois, defending those charged with crimes and non-custodial parents with child support issues.

Marqua is an avid reader, distance bicyclist, roller skater and mentor. A divorcee, she has one daughter, Raigan Billingsley. Marqua's first novel, a political thriller tentatively entitled First Alert, is near completion.

Marqua can be contacted at:
Novel314@aol.com

Mike Beckett –

Mike Beckett is a husband, a father, a software engineer, a writer, a reader, a gamer, and an overall lover of fiction in all its many forms.

During his illustrious 4-year career in the U.S. Navy, Mike served on the USS GEORGE WASHINGTON (CVN-73), whose maiden voyage was a deployment to the exotic Persian Gulf. This experience taught Mike three things: a) traveling is great, b) traveling in America is greater, and c) traveling to an American college is greatest of all.

In one such American college, Mike found a new love: software programming. He took his first C++ course and was hooked for life. And best of all: employers would pay him to do this. An IT job soon followed.

While working that IT job, and while attending his local Southern Baptist church, Mike met an even greater love: his future wife. Marital bliss, and kids, soon followed.

Right about this time, Mike's creative juices starting brewing. He'd been productive with software and productive with a family; now he wanted to be productive with fiction, a long-time love of his. Many stories (and drafts, and redrafts) soon followed.

These days, when Mike isn't writing code, playing with kids, or reminiscing on the good ol' Navy days, he's writing crazy stories about 13th-Century alien monks or 21st-Century ghost dogs. He's sure a book or two is soon to follow.

Mike can be contacted at:
MrTheophilos@yahoo.com

Jennifer Shew –

A lifelong resident of St. Louis, Jennifer is a research technician at the Washington University School of Medicine. She has a degree in biomedical engineering and both her parents are artists, so naturally she has a fondness for writing fantasy. Her parents wanted to make sure she liked reading, and they succeeded. It's their fault that she has read, in a conservative estimate, 1200 books in the last ten years. That's enough to make her think she could write her own.

She began "writing" illustrated stories in first grade and had her first "bestseller" in a fifth grade publishing workshop. She's still waiting for the next one. For the past three years, she has participated in National Novel Writing Month, completing the 50,000-words-in-30-days goal each time. Her muses can be found at etoiline.com.

Jennifer can be contacted at:
etoiline@etoiline.com

P. Anthony Mast –

"First, I was born, which goes without saying..." – Bugs Bunny

Tony is a husband and father. He works days as a database developer and nights as a writer, editor, producer and podcaster. He can currently be heard on The Fanboy Smackdown (www.fanboysmackdown.com), The SciFi Smackdown (www.scifismackdown.com) and Tony's Losing It (www.tonyslosingit.com). He is also working on adapting a short story into a script for a play and completing his first novel.

Tony can be contacted at:

tony@mastville.com